For the first time since *The* returns to London for the back

Artie wanted a dog, but you Fairbright, the block of flats i̶ other animals for that matter. The blue cat Artie found in a tree was unlike any other he had ever seen. Even though he still thought dogs were better, with the help of a nice piece of rock salmon Artie lured it down and, cradling it in his arms, he took it home. His family knew he wouldn't be able to keep it long but they were tolerant towards 'Bluey', as the boy called it, until Artie's mother found the advertisement:

> 'Reward offered. Valuable Russian Blue cat lost since Thursday. Answers to the name of Sacha. Please ring such and such a number with any information.'

Artie knew then that he had lost the cat. But a terrible accident changed everything and the small boy's life became a growing mixture of deception and devotion as he struggled to keep the truth from the owner and his parents and, at the same time, with the help of loyal friends, look after precious 'Bluey' that he had grown to love.

Russian Blue is both exciting and moving and with its vivid background and endearing hero it is one of Helen Griffiths' most appealing stories.

HELEN GRIFFITHS
Russian Blue

Illustrated by Victor Ambrus

HUTCHINSON OF LONDON

HUTCHINSON JUNIOR BOOKS LTD
3 Fitzroy Square, London W1

London Melbourne Sydney Auckland
Wellington Johannesburg Cape Town
and agencies throughout the world

First published 1973

© Helen Griffiths 1973
Illustrations © Hutchinson Junior Books 1973

*This book has been set in Baskerville type, printed in Great Britain
on cartridge paper by Anchor Press, and
bound by Wm. Brendon, both of Tiptree, Essex*

ISBN 0 09 114560 0

For my daughter Elena, fan and critic

Contents

1	Introducing Artie	9
2	The cat	18
3	Bluey	27
4	Saturday and Sunday	35
5	Cat in a bag	42
6	Collision with a car	49
7	Abby	59
8	The shed	68
9	Mrs Bradley	75
10	In the garden	85
11	Betrayal	95
12	Pursuit	107
13	Rain and weariness	115
14	Bluey alone	127
15	Sacha again	137

1. Introducing Artie

Arthur Shaw, better known to his family and acquaintances as Artie or Art, had lived all of his ten and a quarter years in the south-west district of London, near the River Wandle. Artie, who was always very explicit, would confess that he had once gone to a summer camp for two weeks but, except for this, had never lived anywhere else.

He lived on the third floor of a block of flats called The Fairbright Estate. There was nothing either fair or bright about the soot-soiled bricks, the broken communal windows, the smashed courtyard lamps, the consistently despoiled nameplates and the dreary staircases which had been painted half yellow, half brown in the year of Artie's birth and which hadn't seen a paintbrush since. Artie didn't notice the grimness of the place, he was so used to it, and as far as he was concerned he found his surroundings both varied and entertaining.

The Fairbright, as it was locally known, was a world in itself of comings and goings, scandals and joys; then there was the Wandle, which years ago might have contained fish and even frogs and tadpoles, but whose grey, stinking froth had long ago poisoned anything living within its waters. But if you climbed over the park railings and got carefully down the steep bank, preferably wearing Wellingtons and not bothering too much about smells, you could find any number of inanimate objects of unlimited interest and speculation.

Or you could get a bus and go down to Tooting Market on a Saturday morning, to watch eels have their heads chopped off and, if you had the money in your pockets, to buy a jampot full of the grey and white jellied mass the old woman made of them. Your nose would prickle at the smell of all the spices the Pakistanis put in their dinners and your mouth would water at the sight of someone covering a hot dog with lots of tomato sauce and mustard. You could hang about the petshops, where there were terrapins and budgies and the tangy smell of new leather leads and collars, and kid yourself that you were really interested in buying the dog or rabbit food because you had one of these animals at home.

There was always a crowd on the pavement of Balham High Street, milling about a man in its centre whom Artie rarely saw but who was obviously selling something of consuming interest, until a policeman came along, when he always rushed away with his suitcase half open under his arm, mingling among the bystanders whose attention he had been engaging.

But Artie's favourite place was the common, not the most frequented parts where the grass was well tended and there were wooden benches for people to sit on, but beyond, where the common gave up all pretence of being anything other than a stretch of open land. There was a wilderness of rough grass, hummocks, small ponds, trees, bushes, ferns and wild flowers. Footpaths cutting through this wilderness gave the only sign that this was indeed 'common' land, where anyone could walk at will. Out in the real countryside, as Artie knew from his two weeks experience at a summer camp, such footpaths hardly existed.

If you had a dog, the common was the best place he knew of, far better than the park where you weren't supposed to let a dog off the lead. Artie would have let his dog off the lead. The poor thing would want to have a run round after being cooped up in a flat all day. He wanted to run after he'd been in school all day and he knew his dog would feel the same. On the common you could let your dog dig up the dandelions and scratch up the earth and no one minded a bit, but where was the park where you could do that?

Artie often said to his mother, 'Mum, why can't we live somewhere else? If we 'ad a 'ouse wiv a garden we could 'ave a dog, couldn't we?'

But she didn't seem to care if he had a dog or not and

just grumbled something about, 'Too many kids already.'.

A boy at school gave him a brown and white mouse. He called it Nibbles and it lived in his pocket for a week. No one knew about the mouse but his brother Jeff. At night when they were in bed and Davie and Jason were asleep, Artie would get out the mouse and they'd play with it. They made roads and tunnels in the blankets and let it run in and out of their pyjamas. At night Nibbles slept in Artie's pyjama pocket and lived up to his name by nibbling quite a few holes in it. But one morning in the classroom he forgot he had Nibbles in his jacket pocket and, sitting down rather suddenly, squashed it dead.

He and Jeff buried it in the park the following day, Artie twitching his freckled nose with emotion because he felt very bad about what had happened. By the time Jeff had covered it over and pressed down the loose soil with his boot, and made a cross out of two sooty twigs tied together with a long grass stem, he felt a bit better and regret only returned to him that night when it was no good making any more blanket hills and valleys for Nibbles to hurry about in.

The man in the fish-and-chip shop gave him a tortoise. He called it Flash and kept it in a box under his bed until one day he took Flash to the common to give it a treat – eating grass and having a good wander round. He forgot to watch it, only for a minute, but when he looked again it had disappeared. He looked everywhere for it, scratching his skinny legs and arms in the bushes, dragging a few new holes in his pullover. He kept on searching until the sun dipped behind the trees and there were too many shadows for him to make out a tortoise shape, but Flash was gone and that was that.

Artie was always pretending that he had a dog because it was the biggest dream of his life. He was going to have a dog one day, when he was grown up and could do as he liked. Meanwhile, as being grown up was still quite some way off, when he went to the park he would sometimes pretend that the dog was with him.

'Come on, Freddie. Off you go. No nosy old park-keeper around to tell you off,' and the imaginary dog would race off with wagging tail, looking back every now and again as dogs do, to see if he was coming.

Freddie was black and white, big enough for Artie's hand to smooth along his back without having to bend. His tail was long and curly, his eyes were a soft brown, and his pink tongue was always hanging out and dripping everywhere.

Artie watched the dogs in the park. Nearly every day he saw the same ones and he stroked and talked to as many as he could. Freddie, of course, was jealous, especially of the fat, old beagle who wandered about there all by himself in defiance of the notice about dogs being kept on a lead. He didn't seem to belong to anyone and he played with all the dogs and children who took a bit of notice of him.

Several people came with Golden Labradors. There were Alsatians and a Boxer and a dog just like Lassie, and from time to time someone brought a Poodle or a Dachshund. There were lots of mongrels, of course, and these Artie liked best, probably because they were rarely obedient and scarcely trained to anything. They just enjoyed themselves, being dogs, sniffing about and wagging their tails. With his dim view of authority, Artie couldn't help but warm to their independent spirit. They were just like his Freddie.

Artie knew the names of all the different breeds of dogs and if he sometimes made a mistake in identification he was unaware of it. He knew them all because a teacher at school had given him a book which had a photograph of every known breed in the world. It was the only book Artie had because reading was a form of torture as far as he was concerned and if he treasured this one book it was because it was filled with photos and because it was all about dogs.

He couldn't properly read the names of all the dogs in the book. Words like 'Pyrenean Mountain Dog', 'Dobermann', 'Schnauzer' or 'Papillon' were beyond his scope, but his brother Jeff had read them all to him so many times that he knew them by memory. The letters might stump him but his memory never failed.

Artie didn't have a dog because at the Fairbright you weren't allowed to keep animals. Sometimes people broke the rules and then they got into trouble with Mr Bryce, the rent-collector. If they had a dog they would try to have it out somewhere before he came, or if they had a cat they would hide it under the bed or in the toilet. But there were always mean people who would tell on them because they were jealous, or because they'd had a row the week before. And then the dog or cat would have to go. There was no nonsense about that.

*

There were nine children in Artie's family but the only one he really cared about was Jeff who was a year younger than himself. They were almost twins with the same gingery hair, faces lost in freckles, eyes neither blue nor grey but somewhere between the two, and slightly protruding teeth. Jeff was plumper than Artie because he couldn't run about so much. Except for this they could hardly be told apart, with trousers that were too long and had to be constantly hitched up and jerseys that were too short or full of holes.

Jeff sometimes went to the park with Artie. It was quite a good park with plenty of swings and iron poles and a slide as high as the trees. There was a boat made of bricks, concrete posts you could jump over, and a swimming pool that only cost six pence and where you could spend the whole day. Of course, you could only swim when it was warm, even then the water was shivery, but you could go in the paddling pool for nothing if you didn't mind having to put up with all the toddlers.

Artie didn't take Jeff to the common because of his leg. It was only a plastic one. The real one had been smashed under a lorry when he was five. Jeff could swim all right. They had fine times together at the pool in the summer, but he was no good for walking.

Artie admired Jeff in his simple, straightforward way, and whenever he made plans for when he was grown up, like being an R.S.P.C.A. inspector, or a sailor, or a moon explorer, Jeff was always included. They planned to go all round the world together as soon as they'd saved enough money, and Jeff said he might be a smuggler, hiding diamonds or watches inside his leg. They were going to live in a caravan in the country and have lots of animals which Artie would look after because Jeff wasn't so fond of them as he was, and if they went to the moon Jeff would look after all the technical things because he was good at reading and sums, while Artie explored for minerals and unimagined treasures.

Artie didn't spend a lot of time at home if he could help it. There was nothing welcoming in the overcrowded rooms, littered with dirty clothes, unwashed plates, beer bottles, toys and football coupons. He helped himself to some bread and jam after school then went off to the park with Jeff, or on his own, and didn't come home again till supper time.

Supper was often a trip down to the fish-and-chip shop with ten pence in his pocket because his mother was out at Bingo and hadn't stopped to cook anything. She'd won the plaster Alsatians at Bingo and most of the cups and plates.

Once she came home with fifty pounds and on the Saturday they all went down to Tooting and spent the lot, a bike for Jason, a pram for Julie, flashy clothes for Sheila who was nearly grown up – or at least kidded herself she was. The fifty pounds disappeared very quickly. Artie wanted a budgie in a cage but his mother bought him a pair of football boots instead.

Artie's mother didn't bother much about washing and cleaning or even cooking. She was never around when you wanted her and when she did happen to be at home, having run out of money to put in the fruit machines at the local cafés or it being too early for the Bingo club to be open, all she did was tell him to clear out.

As for his father, Artie hardly ever saw him. When he'd had his tea of an evening he would go over to the pub until closing time. On Sundays he stayed in bed till two o'clock, unless there was a football match up on the common. When he talked it was usually to shout at someone and his hand was hard as iron if it caught you around the ear. He figured so little in Artie's life that it was almost as if he didn't even exist.

It was hardly surprising that Artie spent most of his time out of doors. There was nothing at home to draw him to it, no warmth, no comfort, no sense of belonging. He belonged in the streets, in the park, on the common, where he could talk to himself, out loud if he wanted to, and go his own way.

His dog was there, as real to him as a flesh and blood animal, with dancing gaze and eager paws, a combination of all the dogs that most boys dreamed of. His dog was more real than runny-nosed Julie and slouching Phil, more real in his heart than the parents who lived in their own world and had abandoned him to his, and not even the rent-collector could take it away from him.

2. The cat

One evening in July when Artie was meandering home from the park he found a cat. It was almost ten o'clock and there were hardly any people about, except round the pub doors which were open because it was so warm. Several people had brought their drinks outside and Artie felt thirsty at the sight of them. He had eaten five pence worth of chips an hour earlier, with too much salt and vinegar, but in spite of his thirst he didn't feel like going home.

It was just the right sort of night for strolling around the quiet back streets, most of whose little terraced houses were brightly painted and had flowers in tubs or neat hedges beneath their windows. Behind the lace curtains you could make out the shapes of people watching television, or talking and laughing together. Artie was irresistibly drawn towards these homely scenes. Sometimes he felt that if his family lived in a similar house, things would somehow be better. At least he could have a dog because most of the people in these back streets had one.

He came to a corner where the house was boarded up with corrugated tin. Behind the big, silvery-grey sheets were blackened bricks and burned window-frames and a shamble of broken stairways. Last bonfire night a group of boys had broken into the empty building and set it on fire. No one was hurt because the neighbours had called the fire brigade before the flames could spread, but for a long time the house stood damp and abandoned to whoever fancied rummaging about in it. Artie had been inside several times, until an old tramp frightened him off. A smell of burning pervaded the very walls and there was dirt and water everywhere.

Then the council boarded it up because whoever it belonged to didn't seem to care, and for the last few months it had stood there unmolested, bleak, desolate, its only saving grace the almond tree that still flowered in the walled back garden and which was now heavy with long green leaves.

Artie halted at the street corner, looking up at the sky to see if he could see the Great Bear the teacher had been talking about that day. He had never noticed so many stars before, probably because he hadn't bothered to look, and the few clouds looked like cotton-wool patches.

A plaintive mew broke in on his reverie and he looked about, suddenly alert. He couldn't see a cat anywhere but he had definitely heard one and the sound touched a special place inside him because it seemed a cry of need.

'Puss, puss', he tentatively called, not wanting to frighten the cat but hoping it would answer him.

The mew came again, from somewhere behind him. A few yards away a car was parked. Perhaps it was underneath, afraid to come out. Cautiously he approached and knelt down. He could hardly see, because the street lamp threw his shadow in front of him, but he didn't think the cat was there.

There was the cry again! Surely it came from the boarded up house. Perhaps it had got in through a crack somewhere and couldn't find its way out.

'Puss, puss. Where are you? I'm coming. I'll 'elp you. Puss. Puss.'

Once more, the same unhappy sound. Now that he was right beside the house he was sure the sound came from outside. Determined to find the cat, Artie drew as close as he could, trying to peep behind the corrugated boardings, listening with ears that tingled with anticipation but hearing nothing.

Why did the silly thing stop calling? If only it would keep on crying he would soon find it. He paced up and down beside the wall, jumping up every now and then although it was impossible to see over the top. He would get inside the place somehow. He just couldn't ignore that cry of help, and he forgot all about the time. He realized that if he put one foot on the neighbour's low front wall he could, with an effort, pull himself up onto the wall of the damaged house. Once he was there, he jumped down into the garden, where it was suddenly darker and smelled differently to the street. Somehow it even seemed colder and he involuntarily shivered.

'Puss, puss,' he whispered encouragingly, afraid to raise his voice in case some nosy-parker should be watching the street from behind her curtain. It was a local pastime. If anyone saw a shadow in the deserted garden, or heard a noise, they might call the police and then he'd be in trouble. But he was getting fed up with that stupid cat. Did it need help, or didn't it?

A sharp hiss somewhere above him startled him. The blood rushed through his veins for a few seconds until he suddenly realized. Of course! It was up in the tree. There were so many leaves that he couldn't see it. But what a way of scaring someone!

He drew close to the tree trunk and with some effort made out the form of the cat, sitting in the uppermost branches and looking calm and comfortable enough.

'So there you are! Come on down. Can't you get down? Are you stuck?'

There was a sympathetic grin on his freckled face but if the cat could see his expression it was certainly not impressed. After a few moments it repeated the unhappy mew which had urged Artie to action. It was a short, almost apologetic sound.

Artie had never climbed a tree. He'd climbed plenty of iron railings and had a scar on his arm to prove it, and where the sharp spiked fences might deter many a country boy, this sooty, frail-limbed almond tree challenged all his courage. He circled round it a couple of times, still hoping at the bottom of his heart that the cat wasn't really stuck and would come down when it felt like it. He didn't quite know where to start climbing. The lowest branches were well above his head and didn't look very strong. In comics and cartoon films people were always falling out of trees.

He screwed up his nose and scratched the tuft of hair on his forehead, then he saw the battered, rusty washing machine by the wall and with a great deal of puffing and gasping dragged it up against the trunk. He climbed onto the machine, which wobbled precariously, and was able to pull himself without much difficulty into the lowest fork.

The cat wasn't so far away really. Why couldn't it come down by itself. It was watching him with intense interest and its pricked ears looked long and sharp in the moonlight.

'I'll be wiv you in a tick,' promised Artie, more to encourage himself than the cat, and with fast-beating heart pulled himself up to the branch above his head. The tree began to tremble. It wasn't very strong, but the cat was hardly more than a reach away.

Artie stretched upwards, slowly, cautiously, his back pressing against the scratchy trunk, his plimsolled feet half twisted on the slim branch, his tongue licking nervously about his suddenly dry lips. A quick glimpse of the jumbled garden beneath him told him it was a long way off. He kept his gaze on the cat so as not to think about it.

His fingers couldn't quite reach the branch where the cat was perched. It had risen to all fours and was lashing its tail, watching his efforts with unfriendly aspect. Perhaps it didn't want to come down after all. If it had any sense it would jump into his arms.

'Come on, cat. We can't mess about 'ere all night.' His tone was nearly desperate.

The cat hissed and its hair stuck out all over its back, exaggerated by the moonlight. Its front paws minced on the branch as if it couldn't decide what to do and the leaves moved as if the ground were trembling. Artie dared reach no further. Half an inch more and he would crash into the garden. His feet kept slipping and perspiration was trickling down his back.

At last the cat seemed to realize that he was there to help. It stopped hissing, at least, and its hair flattened out again. It crouched and stretched, crouched and stretched, as if intending to jump into Artie's outstretched arms but too uncertain to do so. In the end Artie, who was just as nervous, made a grab at the lashing tail and tugged it towards him, but the cat resisted frantically, digging its claws into the branch it was clinging to and tearing with its back legs at Artie's hand.

Artie let out a cry, the cat let out a yowl, and they both crashed to the ground beneath the tree. For a few seconds Artie was too stunned to move. When he could think, he began to wonder how many bones must be broken, and when his mind was no longer so cloudy he realized that he wasn't really hurt at all. As for the cat, it was still held prisoner by its tail. It crouched in the semi-darkness, glaring at him with baleful expression, ready to run at the first opportunity. Artie was impressed by the savageness of its eyes.

'Puss, puss,' he began softly, trying to coax away the

wildness. 'Don't be scared. I won't 'urt you. 'Aven't I just saved you from that tree?'

The cat yowled threateningly in its throat. The soft menace was enough for Artie, whose hand was beginning to sting and throb.

'Go on you dopey thing. Wish I 'adn't bovvered about you.'

He let go of the tail and, in one bound, the cat was up in the tree again.

Artie gave a disgusted exclamation. 'All that work for nuffink! I might a broke my neck.'

He got up and stared into the foliage. The cat wasn't so high this time but it hissed at the sight of him. Artie sighed and decided to go home.

*

The next day when he came out of school Artie decided to pass by the burned-out house. He didn't really expect the cat to be there still but was curious, just in case. . . . Jeff had gone to the library with his class so he was on his own, and he broke into a run, suddenly anxious, just as if getting there two minutes earlier would make all the difference.

No one noticed him climb into the garden. There was a little brown boy sitting with his feet in the gutter, but his attention was caught by the pigeons who were gulping down the chunks of bread he threw to them.

The almond tree seemed much smaller with the sunlight dappling its leaves. Artie leaned his hand against the trunk and looked up, almost startled when the same cat stared back at him, its muzzle drawn back into a silent snarl.

'What! You still 'ere, mate? You must be daft. But don't kid yourself I'm coming up for you. You'll 'ave to get down by yourself.'

The cat watched him with pricked ears. It didn't seem so frightened after listening to Artie's words. It was an unusual looking animal, quite unlike any cat he had ever seen before and, without knowing anything about them, he realized that this cat was different to the usual run of tabbies and gingers and black-and-white felines that hid under privet bushes or sat watching him from garden walls. Its vivid green eyes were wide apart and foreign-looking, not a bit round as cats' eyes usually were, and contrasting sharply with the deep blue of its thick, shining coat. Its head was narrow and snake-like, its body was long and slim, and its legs looked unusually long too.

'Cor!' he exclaimed, taking in all these details. 'I've really found somefink 'ere. A blue cat wiv green eyes. You don't look real,' he went on, addressing the cat. 'What's your name? Tibbles? No, they wouldn't call you Tibbles. Let's fink.' He twitched his nose. ''Ow about Bluey? Bluey, Bluey, 'Ere Bluey.'

The cat just looked at him, no longer hostile. In fact it seemed quite curious.

'Come on down then. I'm not going to 'urt you. Didn't I try to rescue you last night? And I got into trouble with my Dad for getting 'ome late. And look, just look at my 'and.'

He held his hand up for the cat's inspection. There were two deep scratches and several minor ones running from fingers to wrist and the skin all about was bright red.

'Look what you did, you old misery.'

But he wasn't angry. On the contrary, he was enjoying himself, talking to the cat as if it were his. It was better than talking to Freddie and he could see that the cat was beginning to like the sound of him.

'Come on then, come on down. If you come 'ome wiv me, I'll find you somefink to eat. Just see if I don't. And if there isn't anyfink at 'ome, I'll get some fish up at the fish-and-chip shop. You'll like that, won't you? Come on then. Puss, puss.'

He stayed talking for quite some time but the cat remained unmoving. It listened to him, its long ears twitching from time to time – everything about it was long – but none of his coaxing would bring it down from the branch. Artie could hear shouts of children in the street. They had organized a game of football or something. Now he wouldn't be able to get out of the garden without being seen.

He was afraid for the cat. If someone saw him climb out of the garden they might get in after he had gone to find out what he had been doing there. They might frighten the cat or, even worse, hurt it. Artie didn't trust anybody where animals were concerned.

He went back to the tree and said, 'Listen, puss, I've got to go 'ome for my tea. I'm getting 'ungry, see. But when I come back I'm going to bring you somefink to eat. I'm going to put it down 'ere,' he patted the earth at the foot of the tree, 'and if you're 'ungry, you'll 'ave to come down for it.'

The ball game had moved up to the far end of the street, and, if he were quick, they wouldn't notice him. He grazed his knee as he jumped down to the pavement but whistled airily, with his hands in his pockets, as he looked sharply from side to side to see if someone might be spying on him.

He could see no one at the windows. The little brown boy had gone and so had the pigeons, scared away by the football, and he felt easier. As soon as he turned the corner, he set off at a run, wanting to get back to the cat as soon as he could, already planning how he was going to look after it and even take it home if he could. Perhaps if it hadn't cost him anything his Mum wouldn't mind, or perhaps he and Jeff could keep it secret like the tortoise. But first he had to get it out of the tree and gain its confidence, and a bit of rock salmon from the fish-and-chip shop would be the best thing for that.

3. Bluey

More than an hour had gone by when Artie returned to the cat in the tree. He could hardly believe his luck in finding it there still, having expected it to have gone home long since. He was under the impression that cats were sensible animals, even if they did get stuck in trees sometimes, but perhaps this one was lost and stayed in the tree because it felt safest there.

He was already thinking of a name for it while he waited at the fish-and-ship shop. He was the first customer and the Italian hadn't any fish ready because not many people asked for it at five o'clock.

He still didn't know if it was a he or a she so he couldn't give it a boy's or girl's name until he found out. Had it been a tabby cat he would have called it Tiger. He'd always wanted to have a striped cat and call it Tiger, but this one was a funny, blue sort of colour. Fancy, a blue cat! He'd have to tell Jeff but he bet Jeff wouldn't believe him. He himself wouldn't have believed anyone if they said they'd seen a blue cat, and he recalled the name he had thought of that afternoon. Bluey. Yes, Bluey was all right. It could be a he or a she with that name, it wouldn't matter. And Bluey really suited it because that's what it was like.

The fish was still burning his finger tips through the greaseproof and newspaper when he climbed over the wall into the garden, softly calling, 'Bluey, Bluey. Are you still there?'

Cautiously he approached the tree, not wanting to frighten the cat this time, and heaved a sigh of relief when he found it hadn't disappeared.

'Come on, Bluey. Come on down. Look what I got for you.'

He screwed up his eyes to look at the cat, for the sun slanting through the leaves almost blinded him, and it

looked as though it almost welcomed him in the way it pricked its ears and twitched its tail.

He knelt at the foot of the tree and unwrapped the paper. A lovely smell of fried fish and hot batter hit him, making him feel hungry, but he reminded himself that Bluey must be a lot hungrier if he'd been in the tree all night, and perhaps longer! Who knew how long he'd been there?

Gingerly he pulled the fish out of the grease-proof bag.

'Ouch! It's 'ot. Come on down, Bluey. Can't you smell it? It's a smashing bit of fish.'

He broke it up into small pieces, burning his fingers, licking the grease off them and popping just a couple of battery bits into his mouth. He spread it all out so that Bluey could see it plainly, then moved away in case he was afraid to come down while he was near.

He was just beginning to wonder if he ought to climb the tree a second time when Bluey stood up, ears pricked, nose twitching, hesitatingly looking for a way down. His tail-tip flicked nervously, confirming Artie's opinion that the lovely fish smell was irresistible and that the cat would get down to it somehow or another.

For all that he was watching closely he didn't see how Bluey got down, so effortless was the movement which brought him right beside the newspaper to sniff and jerk his head away, then sniff again, excited but unsure.

Artie didn't move. He hardly even breathed. Now the cat was down, he could just as easily dash over the wall as stay there and then he'd be lost for good.

Bluey put one paw onto the newspaper and drew closer to the fish. He looked back at Artie, half suspiciously, his tail tip still flicking, then sniffed again at the offering. Hunger overcame suspicion at last and he crouched down on the paper, gingerly catching a chunk between his

B

teeth, dropping it with hastily shaking head because it was hot, then licking for a second or two before once again taking hold. This time he chewed it up and swallowed it. He took another quick glance at Artie before going on to the next piece and then he forgot the boy while he unhurriedly chewed up bit after bit until he was satisfied.

Meanwhile, Artie watched spellbound, amazed at the cat's careful, tidy way of eating. A boy he knew had a dog and when food was put down for it, big chunks of raw meat, it swallowed it in twenty-five seconds flat without chewing anything. They had timed it between them so he knew.

Bluey didn't eat all the fish. When he'd had enough he sat back and started to lick himself, beginning with his jaws then continuing with his paws, which he wet with his tongue before rubbing them over his eyes and ears. While this was going on, Artie drew closer. The cat stopped for a minute to watch him but made no effort to run away. On the contrary, Artie could hear a purring sound deep down in his throat as he went on licking, licking, licking.

He sat down beside the cat, with only the bit of newspaper between them.

'That was good, wasn't it, Bluey? I bet you really enjoyed it.'

He looked at the paper. There were still a few bits left, the chunky bits which the cat hadn't fancied. It seemed a pity to waste them, especially as it was his supper, so while he waited for Bluey to finish washing himself he ate them up. Bluey took a sniff at his outstretched hand then went on purring and washing. He didn't seem at all afraid now and Artie was puzzled.

Cats were definitely funny things. He'd spent a whole night and best part of the day in the tree, hissing and mewing and refusing to be rescued, and now here he was, as happy as could be, and all because he'd eaten a bit of hot fish. He didn't think dogs were so puzzling, but then he knew a lot more about dogs than cats. He'd never bothered about cats before, except to click his tongue at them when he passed them sitting on walls or between parked cars, because, with his love of dogs, he'd always considered them pretty inferior animals. Perhaps they weren't so bad, after all, at least not this one who looked like a foreign prince.

Artie's cleaning-up process was much quicker than Bluey's. He just rubbed his greasy fingers a couple of times across his shirt front and that was that.

To his surprise the next thing Bluey did was come over to him and start rubbing himself against his arm, still purring and absolutely fearless. Artie began to stroke the glossy blue back and he quickly turned round and rubbed his head under the hand carressing him, eyes shut, long ears flattened against the narrow skull, with an expression of utter contentment.

Soon Artie had the cat on his knees, with the tapered head rubbing against his shirt and under his chin.

'Cor! You like a lot of fuss, don't you, Bluey!' he exclaimed delightedly. 'After being such a misery last night! I suppose you was frightened,' and he stroked and scratched and tickled, forgetting all about the time.

*

Artie decided to take Bluey home. He knew he couldn't keep an animal at the Fairbright but deep inside him was the irrepressible hope that no one would find out and that nothing would be said. Besides, he couldn't leave him in the garden, homeless. Sooner or later something would happen to him, like being run over. . . . For a fleeting moment he considered keeping him in the garden, a secret, but he knew that Bluey wouldn't stay there for ever, waiting for him. He'd wander off, he'd find his way back home, and Artie would never see him again.

Home! Where was Bluey's home anyway? He obviously had a home and someone who took great care of him because he was such an affectionate creature and his coat had almost a glow. Quickly, Artie pushed from his head the thought of Bluey's owner. Bluey belonged to him now. He'd found and rescued him. The only problem was persuading his Mum to let him stay.

It was about seven o'clock when he got home, with Bluey tucked unwillingly inside his shirt, a good time really because there was no one in the courtyards or on the staircase. They were all indoors watching television and finishing their suppers. Artie was hoping that Jeff would share his secret before anyone else found out, but it happened that his mother was home and she was the first person he saw when he got in.

'What you got there, Artie?' she exclaimed.

'Oh, Mum, let me keep 'im. It's a cat I found. It's ever so clean and friendly. Don't say I can't 'ave 'im.'

'You know the rules, Art. It's nothing to do with me. If Mr Bryce sees 'im, out 'e goes, and that's that. No good crying to me afterwards.'

'You mean I can keep 'im!' he cried joyfully.

'You 'eard what I said,' was her non-commital reply. 'Let's 'ave a look at 'im.'

Artie pulled Bluey out of his shirt and put him on the table among the dirty supper plates. Bluey immediately took fright and in one leap had hidden himself under the sideboard.

'Though you said 'e was friendly?'

'Well, 'e is wiv me. I 'spect 'e's a bit scared.'

His mother kneeled down by the sideboard and called,

'Puss, puss,' but Bluey wouldn't come out and he wouldn't even budge when Artie called him.

'Never mind,' said Mrs Shaw. ''E'll come out when 'e's ready.'

Julie, Pat and Jason tried to crawl under the sideboard to get him but Bluey's hisses deterred them and after a few impatient exclamations they left the strange cat alone. Jeff wasn't at home and it wasn't until the younger ones were in bed, his parents and elders out, with the flat more or less in silence that Bluey ventured out from his hiding place.

Artie poured milk into a saucer for him but he didn't drink it. He explored all round the living room, sniffing the chairs and carpet, jumping up on the table to sniff the cloth and twitch his nose at the sauce bottles, and made no protest when Artie took him into his arms and carried him off to his bed.

He was playing with him there, getting his fingers scratched, when Jeff came in.

'Cor! What you got there?'

'What's it look like? A lion? A tiger?' and eagerly he explained how he had found Bluey and all that had happened since then, finishing, 'And Mum's letting me keep 'im. At least, she says I can so long as Mr Bryce don't find out.'

''E's a funny colour,' said Jeff, gently stroking Bluey's chin, and Artie was glad to see that the cat wasn't afraid of him.

'I've called 'im Bluey. What do you fink?'

'If 'e was mine, I'd call 'im Prince. 'E looks like a prince, some'ow.'

'It's a girl,' said Artie, who had only recently made this discovery.

'What do you call 'im ''im' for, then?'

'Don't know,' he shrugged. 'I got used to finking of 'im as 'im but 'e's a girl really.'

'Call 'im Princess then, or Queenie.'

'No!' exclaimed Artie scornfully. 'Mr Archer used to call his old rag-and-bone 'orse Queenie, and look what an ugly fing she was.'

'I bet 'e's worf a lot of money,' said Jeff thoughtfully. 'It's not like 'e was a tabby or somefink. I bet 'e's a show cat or somefink.'

''E's beautiful,' agreed Artie contentedly. 'And ever so friendly.' He saw Jeff look doubtfully at his hands and added, 'Well, 'e's scratched me a bit but only playing.'

'Trouble is,' went on Jeff. 'If 'e's a valuable animal 'is owner'll want 'im back.'

''E'll 'ave a job to find 'im,' replied Artie aggressively. 'I'm not giving 'im up now. 'E's mine. Cats aren't like dogs. You don't 'ave to 'ave licences for 'em. Besides, who's going to know I've got 'im?'

'Don't know,' said Jeff, 'but someone'll find out. They always do. With all the kids in this family, someone's bound to tell.'

'As long as Mr Bryce don't know it don't matter,' argued Artie. 'And 'e's never going to see 'im, I'll make sure of that.'

'Even so . . . ' but he didn't go on.

Artie played with Bluey and Jeff joined in. The cat pounced on their hands and, when they were in bed, whirled about like a mad thing, attacking the toes they wriggled under the bed clothes. Eventually she (because it's about time Bluey was properly recognized as a female) curled up in the space between Artie's chest and arm and, purring gently, fell asleep.

It was like music to Artie and he drifted off into slumber too, his dirty, freckled face creased with happiness.

4. Saturday and Sunday

Artie believed that all his troubles were over, now that he had permission to keep the cat, but he was soon to discover that this was far from the case. To start with, when Bluey woke from her long night's slumber she was immediately unsettled by her strange surroundings. Although the evening before she had accepted Artie's attentions with playful affection, the new day brought with it an instinctive reminder of all her old habits, none of which she could satisfy in this unknown place.

Artie, of course, knew nothing of her ways; how at six in the morning her mistress would bring her downstairs in her arms and let her out through the kitchen door to the garden, where she would stay, chasing her tail, smelling the dew on the lawn and watching with quivering form the short, sharp flights of the birds in the trees and blackberry bushes, until she was called in by the clink of a spoon against a saucer.

Artie had no garden for her to play in and although she pawed hopefully at all the doors in turn, escaping the grasping hands of the younger children, and jumped up to the windows to scratch in distress, there was no way of soothing her anxiety. She seemed to have forgotten the boy's attentions of the previous day and her purring acceptance of him. All she wanted was to satisfy her old habits, and this she could not do.

'What's the matter wiv 'im?' asked Jeff.

'I expect 'e wants to go somewhere,' said Artie knowledgeably.

'Where you going to put 'im then?'

'Don't know. I 'adn't fought about it.'

'A bit of newspaper in a box,' suggested Jeff. 'That's what you're supposed to put. A bit of newspaper. They say cats are very clean.'

Artie ran to the living room for his father's newspaper, which was usually halfway under the armchair, where it always slid when he fell asleep in front of the television at midnight. He tipped Jason's toys out of the cardboard box, leaving them strewn over the carpet, and rushed back to Jeff and Bluey.

''Ere we are. Let's put 'im in.'

Jeff put Bluey in the box on the newspaper and Bluey immediately jumped out again, tail beginning to twitch with annoyance.

''E don't know what it's for,' said Artie. 'Let's try again.'

He caught Bluey and put her back in the box, with the same result.

'P'raps 'e's used to sawdust. You know, that stuff they sell at the petshop.'

'Cor! Well, we can't afford that. 'E'll 'ave to get used to newspaper. I'll tell you what. Later on we'll go up the park and get some earth. 'E might like that better. Maybe 'e's used to a garden.'

'But you can't keep getting earth from the park. It's too 'eavy.'

'Only till 'e gets used to the paper. You'll see. Cats are intelligent. More than dogs.'

Jeff looked in surprise at this statement from his brother. 'I fought you liked dogs best!'

'So I do, but cats is more intelligent.'

'I've never seen a cat do tricks,' argued Jeff doubtfully.

'Cos they can't be bovered with such silly fings. What's a cat want to do tricks for? Come on, let's try and get 'im in the box again.'

The box was a failure, probably because its sides were too high and Bluey distrusted their motives. In the end she satisfied her most urgent need in the big pot of geraniums Mrs Shaw had bought a couple of weeks earlier in Tooting Market. Artie didn't find out until he discovered the bedraggled plant thrown out on the floor, and he pushed it back quickly into the soil before someone else found out too.

It was Saturday that morning, so Artie stayed at home to keep Bluey company and to try to get her used to him. He gave her a saucer of milk, which she didn't like, then the leavings from his bowl of cornflakes which she also despised. He gave her a bit of bread and jam which, after a certain amount of cautious sniffing, she daintily swallowed, licking herself all over afterwards as if to get rid of the stickiness of Artie's fingers which had caressed her all the while.

'Clean, isn't 'e?' said Jeff admiringly. He was keeping both Artie and the cat company. 'What we going to feed 'im on if 'e don't like milk?'

'When Mum gets up we'll ask if we can 'ave some money to buy some cat food. They sell it in tins. I don't suppose she'll mind as she said I could keep 'im. I mean, she must know 'e 'as to eat.'

Jeff nodded agreement.

Bluey didn't like the tinned cat food. She had been brought up on the best minced meat, the best stewed rabbit, chicken breasts and freshly-boiled whiting, and this pinky, strong-smelling stuff out of a tin was quite foreign to her. Artie watched her reaction with dismay.

'Cor! And we bought the big economy size!' he exclaimed. 'Mum won't 'alf be mad if she 'as to chuck it out.'

'P'raps 'e's not 'ungry,' suggested Jeff. ''E didn't want 'is milk this morning neiver, did 'e?'

'Course 'e must be 'ungry. Wouldn't you be 'ungry if you 'adn't 'ad no breakfast and 'ardly anyfing to eat the day before?'

'Well, 'e's not very big. P'raps 'e likes fish best. You said 'e ate that fish yesterday.'

'Tell you what,' said Artie, lowering his voice to a whisper. 'Mum's got some minced meat in 'er bag. She's going to make a cottage pie. What if I pinch a bit? If I don't take much I bet she don't notice.'

Later on, seeing the satisfaction with which Bluey cleaned the meat from the plate, he was sure the risk had been worth while.

In the afternoon, when Mr Shaw woke from his doze and switched on the television to watch the sporting programme, he said, 'This place stinks of cat.'

'Well,' said his wife, 'we got a cat, 'aven't we?'

'I don't need no reminding about that,' he replied bad-temperedly. ''Ow long's it staying 'ere? That's what I want to know.'

'Oh, you're always moaning. Let the boy 'ave 'is cat if 'e wants it. I've told 'im 'e'll 'ave to get rid of it if Mr Bryce 'ears about it.'

'Sooner than that,' threatened Mr Shaw, 'if you don't get rid of this stink.'

Then he forgot about the subject, eyes glued to the flickering screen.

Artie said to Jeff, 'Did you 'ear what Dad said?'

'Yes, but don't take any notice.'

'I wish we could take 'im out.' He sighed. 'One fing about a dog, you can put 'im on a lead and take 'im for walks.'

Bluey was sitting on his bed, emerald eyes staring at the window with the torn lace curtain. Artie had tired of wriggling his fingers because Bluey took no notice.

'P'raps you ought to try and find out who 'e belongs to,' suggested Jeff after a silence. He had been watching Bluey too and saw how the cat's gaze never left that space of sunlight.

''E belongs to me,' retorted Artie determinedly. 'I found 'im and I'm keeping 'im.'

*

Sunday morning was about the only time the whole family had breakfast together, mainly because breakfast wasn't until gone eleven and by then everyone had woken up. Mrs Shaw flapped around the stove and table in a pair of old slippers and an even older dressing gown, whose many stains had become part of the pattern, slapping down eggs and bacon on cracked plates and dishing up tea in thick, blue-and-white-striped mugs.

Mr Shaw was up for once and ate his breakfast hidden behind the newspaper. He was hardly ever seen and when everyone had what they needed his wife also disappeared behind the local news, sipping tea and reading at the same time.

Artie had the cat on his knees. On Sunday Bluey was not quite so restless. Artie had brought earth from the park in Jason's and Julie's sand buckets and solved one problem for the moment, and also the flat was no longer so strange to her. But she was still unhappy, unused to so many people, especially the noisy children who wouldn't leave her alone until Artie gave up threatening and started slapping, and she had realized that her only refuge from all the strange things that both displeased and frightened her was with him.

She accepted a bit of cold bacon from his fingers and a piece of toast soaked with egg yolk, then licked the fat congealing on his plate. Sheila watched with disgust.

'You shouldn't let that animal eat off your plate!'

'Why not? I bet 'e's a good bit cleaner than you. 'E's always washing 'imself, which is more than what you do.'

'You cheeky little——'

'Oh, shut up,' broke in their mother. 'Always quarrelling.'

'Well, look what 'e's doing, Mum. Letting the cat——'

'Leave the cat alone. Always picking on people, you are Sheil. Don't know where you get your airs and graces.'

'She's jealous, cos it ain't 'ers,' put in thirteen-year-old Brian, mostly to annoy his sister, and Sheila slammed out after sticking her tongue out at half the family.

There was silence for a few minutes, except for the noise of eating, then Mrs Shaw exclaimed, ''Ere, listen to this.' She read in an important voice. '"Reward offered. Valuable Russian Blue cat lost since Thursday. Answers to the name of Sacha. Please ring such-and-such a number with any information."'

Everyone suddenly looked at Artie and Bluey.

'Sacha. Sacha,' called Brian in a coaxing voice and the cat pricked her ears.

'It's 'im,' he cried. 'Look 'ow 'e knows 'is name.'

Everyone started calling to Sacha and even Mr Shaw put down his paper for a moment to see the cat's reaction.

'It's 'im all right,' agreed Mrs Shaw. 'Fancy! I wonder 'ow much the reward'll be.'

'I don't want no reward,' cried Artie, scarlet in the face. 'It's my cat now, I found 'im.'

'But you can't keep 'im if 'e belongs to someone else.'

'I bet if there wasn't a reward you wouldn't care. You're only thinking of the reward.'

'And why not? You can get any old cat off the street and it doesn't cost you a tanner. This is a valuable one and it's only right the owner should 'ave 'im back.'

Artie pressed his lips together and clung tightly to Bluey, who was licking at the last bit of fried egg on his plate.

'If 'e's a valuable cat they should look after 'im better. Not let 'im go roaming round the streets. If 'e'd got run over, if 'e was dead, they couldn't 'ave 'im back, could they? Not if 'e was dead they couldn't.'

'But 'e's not dead. 'E's right 'ere and 'e'll 'ave to go back where 'e belongs. You can 'ave a new cat if you want, as long as Mr Bryce don't find out. The woman's cat up at the tea-shop 'as just 'ad kittens.'

Artie said nothing. He pulled Bluey into his arms and marched off to his room. Jeff went after him.

'What are we going to do?' he said.

Artie couldn't speak.

'Course, you could 'ave another one,' Jeff went on consolingly. 'Mum just said so. A kitten. They're more fun than cats. And you can get it used to the newspaper from the start. That'd be better, wouldn't it?'

'Oh, shut up,' snapped Artie. 'You're as bad as Mum. What do I want a kitten for? It wouldn't be as pretty as Bluey, would it? It wouldn't be the same, would it? Do you think I can change cats, just like that, and not notice the difference?'

'Well, you've only 'ad 'im for two days,' Jeff argued reasonably.

'So what? I'm not giving 'im up.'

'You'll 'ave to,' said Jeff. 'You can't keep 'im if 'e's not yours. And if you get the reward, like it says, you can buy them roller skates you wanted.'

'Reward!' Artie almost choked over the word. 'All people think about is money.'

5. Cat in a bag

After breakfast, Mrs Shaw got dressed and put on her coat. The sun was burning in the street but she never went out without her coat, almost as grubby and just as old as the dressing gown. She looked in on Artie and Jeff who were playing with Bluey.

'I'm going to make that phone call,' she said. 'So you'd better stay in just in case when I come back you'll 'ave to take 'im to 'is owner.'

Half an hour later she came back and Artie rushed to the door to meet her, his freckled face unusually pallid.

'Blooming telephone boxes. Never work, they don't. Blinking kids are always smashing 'em up. I've tried three this morning. Three! And not one of 'em working. I lost my money in the last one too, and when I told the operator she didn't believe me. Post Office can get rich all right on all the lost cash that goes in them boxes.'

'So you 'aven't phoned then?' Artie sighed with relief.

'No, but I'll get your Dad to do it when 'e goes over to the pub. They'll let 'im use the phone there. That'll be working at least.'

But Mr Shaw forgot to make the call and Artie felt safe for that day at least. His main fear was that while he was at school the following day, his mother might take the cat back herself. If only he could hide Bluey somewhere!

A lot of ideas went through his head, like taking her back to the deserted house, or putting her high up in the tree again until the danger was past, but he dismissed them as impractical. He was afraid to leave Bluey alone somewhere, in case she escaped, and he was also afraid of being seen with her inside the Fairbright. The courtyard was always crowded with children on a Sunday and someone would be bound to see him with Bluey.

He spent the whole of Sunday indoors with his cat and Bluey delighted him with her way of rubbing up against him, arching her slender back, purring deeply. She even licked his hand, her sandpaper tongue bringing a grin of contentment to him.

'Look, Jeff,' he cried. 'Look 'ow 'e licks me. Just like a dog. Just shows I ought to keep 'im. 'E loves me already.'

'P'raps 'e just likes the taste of you,' suggested Jeff who hadn't been licked.

But she nuzzled him too and fell asleep on Artie's lap while he watched a film on the television, a bit of his jersey caught between her front teeth which she sucked while she slept. Artie hardly noticed the film, engrossed by Bluey's soft warmth and the sensation of utter contentment that filled him. He had never been so still in all his life as he was that afternoon with the Russian Blue curled against his stomach.

The following day he was loath to go to school. It was the beginning of the last week. On Friday the holidays began. What a pity they hadn't started already and he could stay with Bluey all day long.

His mother was still in bed when he set out for school. He left Bluey in his room with the door tightly shut, the box with the earth in a corner by the window. He had put down a saucer of milk and a chunk of the tinned cat food on a plate beside it, and had left an old tennis ball for Bluey to play with. Before he went he had fondled and stroked the cat as if he were never going to see her again, and all day he could think of nothing else.

*

When he came home from school, and before he could

even see Bluey, his mother said, "Well, Art, you'll have to take 'im back. I've been on to 'is owner today, a Mrs Bradley, and I told 'er you'd take 'im round just as soon as you got 'ome.'

'But Mum——!'

'She said she'd come 'ere for 'im, but I didn't want that. Don't want strangers nosing around 'ere.'

'But——'

'She said to put 'im in a box and make sure 'e can't get out, just in case 'e's frightened by the traffic, so I got a box from the grocers and 'ave already made a couple of 'oles in it, so 'e can breathe all right.'

'But Mum, 'ow could you? You said I could keep 'im.'

'Now, Art, we've already been over this. I said 'e's to go back. Your Dad's already complaining about 'im. And you 'aven't seen yet what 'e's done to the curtain in your room.'

'It was torn anyway. 'As been for monfs,' he argued sulkily.

'I asked 'er what the reward was,' his mother went on, ignoring him, 'and she said five pounds if it really is 'er cat. She lives up by the common, in one of them big 'ouses with the gardens in front.'

Artie said nothing. There was nothing he could say. His heart seemed to choke in his throat. There was the box on the table with the holes punched in it. 'Baked Beans' it said. Mrs Shaw saw what he was looking at.

'I only 'ope it's strong enough,' she said. 'It's a long way up to the common. Do you want to get the bus? We could tie a bit of string round it, I suppose.'

'Do I 'ave to take 'im, Mum? Couldn't I keep 'im a bit longer? Just a day. Just till tomorrow.'

'It'll be your five pounds, Artie. I'll put it in the Post Office for you or buy some Premium Bonds. You might win twenty-five thousand if you're lucky, though if you have your Dad's luck with the 'orses, you won't get nothing.'

Artie wasn't listening. He moved away and went to find Bluey. The room smelled of cat and stale food as he opened the door, a tangy, sickly smell that made his nose twitch. Bluey was asleep on his bed, stretched out on her back with her paws half in the air, her narrow head hanging down, almost touching the lino. He pulled her into his arms, her softness enveloping him as he hugged her against his face. She didn't struggle to free herself but put up a smooth, oval paw against his cheek.

'It's not fair,' he muttered. 'It's not fair. Who wants rotten old Premium Bonds anyway?'

He sat on the bed and fondled Bluey. She immediately wanted to play and pounced on his knees, digging her claws into the flesh and hurting him. Her stiff tail whipped back and forth right under his nose, tickling him and making him laugh in spite of his growing misery.

'Come on, Artie,' called his mother from the living room. 'Don't waste time. Get 'im in the box. I told the woman you'd be there about five and she's waiting for you.'

'Give us somefink to eat first. I'm 'ungry.'

She sliced a chunk of bread from the big loaf and smeared it with butter and strawberry jam.

'Where's Jeff?' she said. ''E can go with you if you take the bus.'

'I 'spect 'e'll be along in a minute. I came running. Wanted to see Bluey, just in case . . . '

Jeff came in while he was finishing the hunk of bread and he waited while he had a slice too.

'Come on, you two,' scolded their mother sharply. 'You're just wasting time. You, Art, get that cat and stick it in the box. I'll 'old the lid ready, in case it tries to jump out.'

Putting Bluey into the box was easy enough. Keeping her there was the difficult part. Even though Mrs Shaw managed to get the two flaps down, Bluey was already pushing her head free and, in half a second, squeezed her body through the incredibly small space, in spite of Mrs Shaw's pushing, grasping hands and determination. She flew under the sideboard, she dived under the armchair, she jumped up on the mantelpiece and almost knocked down the clock.

'For 'eaven's sake!' yelled Mrs Shaw at last, red faced, her untidy hair more disordered than ever. 'Leave the thing alone till it calms down a bit. It'll 'ave our eyes out in a minute. Just as well you are taking it back. Vicious thing. I don't want it around 'ere with little Jason and Julie.'

These two came in as she spoke and added to the confusion by trying to catch Bluey in spite of her screeched exhortations to leave her alone. She hit Jason round the ear, pulled Julie's hair, and there was a chorus of wails and screams which unnerved the excited cat even more.

'I've got an idea,' cried Mrs Shaw at last. 'Jeff, you get my big shopping bag from the kitchen. You know the one. That tartan one with the zip. If we can get 'im in there and zip 'im up 'e'll 'ave a job to get out, I can say.'

'But Mum, 'e won't be able to breav in there!' exclaimed Artie.

'Course 'e will. It's not as if 'e's going to be there long. Not above 'alf an hour if you get a move on and go on the bus.'

'But it'll be all dark.'

'So what? 'E won't die, will he? You just do as I say if you don't want a clout round the ear like Jason. I'm fed up to the back teeth with this cat of yours. And don't bring any more animals 'ome, if you know what's good for you.'

After another struggle, in which Artie got a scratch from his wrist to his elbow, Bluey was imprisoned inside the tartan shopping bag and firmly zipped up. Yowls and miaows and long, frantic wails issued from it, accom-

panied by violent movements. The top of the zip began to move slightly, so Mrs. Shaw found a bit of string which she threaded through the hole of the zipper and tied to the ring of the bag's handle.

'I'd like to see 'im get that open now,' she said with almost savage satisfaction. 'And don't you think of opening it while you're in the bus, young Artie, or you'll be in trouble. That cat'll be out like a bomb when you do open it.'

Artie picked up the bag. It bumped against his leg and the expression on his face was of deepest concern and misery.

''E'll die in 'ere, Mum. Honest 'e will. 'E'll sufflicate.'

'Let 'im then. As long as you get 'im out of this 'ouse. Well, come on, what are you waiting for?' She brushed the hair out of her eyes crossly.

'The bus fare,' said Jeff, holding out his hand.

Then the two boys went carefully down the stairs and along the street to the bus-stop, Artie biting his lip, Jeff watching the bag. He had the address they were going to on a piece of paper in his pocket, but when he pulled out the five pence to give to the conductor for their fares, it fell onto the floor, unnoticed by either of them. They didn't discover their loss until they were in the street again, walking towards the common, and Artie asked Jeff to get out the paper and tell him where they were going.

'It's gone,' he cried, after he'd nearly pulled his pockets to pieces looking for it. 'Cor blimey! Now what we going to do?'

6. Collision with a car

'Mum won't 'alf be mad,' said Jeff.

'Well, you go back and tell 'er. She never gets so mad wiv you as she does wiv me. If I go, I'll get a clout round the ear'ole.'

'What you going to do while I'm gone?' said Jeff, finding his brother's argument reasonable.

'I'll wait for you 'ere. Look, see where that big tree is? I'll sit on that seat there till you come back.'

'Okay. But don't open the bag, will you? Remember what Mum said.'

'Oh, don't worry. I'm not daft. Go on, then, or it'll be midnight before you're back again.'

Artie watched Jeff hurry back the way they had come. His limp was hardly noticeable, except when he was tired, but he didn't have to walk very far if he took the bus so Artie didn't worry.

When Jeff had turned the corner which led to the main road, Artie picked up the tartan bag and made his way over to the seat beneath the chestnut tree on a corner of the common. There were houses on two sides of this stretch of grass, all of which had been very grand in their time but which were now divided into flatlets. In some the gardens were well-tended still, while in others grass and weeds were growing almost up to the front windows and they were dark with overgrown trees. Perhaps Bluey lived in one of these houses and, for a while, he entertained himself trying to guess which one it might be. Then he tried to imagine what it would be like if one of these big properties belonged to his family. They could have dogs and cats and rabbits, and all sorts of animals if they lived in such a big house and he considered which one he would choose if he won the football pools one day.

The time seemed to go by very slowly in spite of his thoughts. He knew it would take Jeff the best part of half an hour to get back to him, if he didn't have to wait too long for the buses, and he was incapable of sitting still for so long. He looked at the bag which he had placed carefully between his feet. Bluey had been very still for a long time. On the bus she had mewed twice, but he couldn't remember how long it was since she had last uttered a sound or made a movement.

Perhaps he ought to just open the zip a tiny bit so that she could get some fresh air. After all, his mother hadn't expected her to be cooped up for so long. Jeff's warning flashed through his mind but he knew that if he was very careful nothing could happen. He would only open it a tiny, little bit, not enough for her to get her head through. It wasn't as if he were in the street, either. There were a couple of roads behind him, dividing the houses from the common, but hardly any cars went by and they were a good distance from where he was sitting.

For a few minutes Artie fiddled with the knot his mother had tied in the string. Until he undid it, he couldn't open the zip. Bluey remained unmoving, even though he clicked his tongue and called her name, and anxiety grew with his irritation over the knot. At last, with the help of his teeth, he got it undone and then with great care he pulled the zip back half an inch. Bluey's nose was immediately in the tiny opening, pressed against the zip's teeth. An unhappy yowl broke from her.

'Cor! You're still alive then!' exclaimed Artie with relief. 'But stick your nose back in before I zip it up.'

He pushed her nose down with his fingers, intending to pull up the zip which had slipped open a bit further under

Bluey's pressure, but the cat's struggles became more determined and soon her whole muzzle was through the space and Artie was scared of tugging at the zip in case he caught her whiskers in it.

'Get on in,' he said sharply, pushing again, then he jumped back with a cry because Bluey had dug a claw deep into his finger.

Blood welled from the wound, which was quite deep, but Artie hadn't time to notice because the zip was straining against Bluey's frantic pushing. He went to make another effort but, even as he leaned over the bag, Bluey leaped out under his very nose, startling him so that, before he could react, she was loping across the grass towards the road.

''Ere. Come back,' he cried, running after her.

Perhaps she was too frightened to take any notice, or perhaps she knew her way home from here and didn't intend to be prevented from returning. Either way, Artie's pursuit only served to increase her speed. She dashed arrow-like across the road, that road along which so little traffic passed, and Artie gave an agonized cry as the glossy body hurled into the air away from the car that hit her.

Artie was stunned, unable to accept that so much could happen in so short a space of time. Only a few seconds had passed since she jumped from the bag and now she was lying on a patch of grass that grew from beneath a garden wall. He reached her there just as the driver of the car came up.

There was no blood, no mark, but she was either unconscious or dead.

'I'm sorry, young fellow,' said the man concernedly. 'It is your cat, I suppose?'

Artie nodded. He couldn't possibly speak. Tears were sliding down his cheeks but he couldn't utter a sound.

'I saw her dash across the road but couldn't stop in time. You shouldn't have a cat out in the street.'

Artie went down on his knees, stretching out a hand to touch her gently. She was just as warm and soft as ever, only she didn't move and her eyes were closed.

'You've killed 'im.' His voice was hardly more than a groan of despair. 'You've killed 'im.'

'Perhaps not. Let's have a look.'

The man knelt down beside Artie and passed his hand along the length of the cat. 'I don't think she's dead,' he said. 'The best thing is to get her to a vet as quickly as possible.'

Carefully, he picked her up, stretching her along his arm as if he were used to cats. Artie rubbed his sleeve across his face to dry the tears and nodded when the man asked him if he lived nearby.

'Let me take you both back home in my car and then I'll run her down to the vet for you, if you like. I don't mind paying the damages.'

'I'll take 'im,' said Artie, holding out his arms. 'I'll take 'im to the Blue Cross. The bloke there knows me. I won't 'ave to pay nuffink.'

'Well, tell me where it is and I'll pop you down there.'

Artie shook his head. 'I'm waiting for my bruver. 'E'll be 'ere in a minute. I'll go wiv 'im.'

The man ignored his outstretched arms, seemingly unwilling to part with Bluey. 'I don't know whether I ought to——'

''E's mine,' insisted Artie truculently. 'I can look after 'im.'

'That's just it. Can you look after him? You shouldn't have been out with him in the first place. He looks a valuable animal to me. Why don't you let me take him to a vet? It wouldn't take long in the car.'

But he saw the distrust in Artie's face and, with a sigh, put the cat in his arms. He took out his wallet and pulled a pound note from it. 'This should cover the cost of the treatment.'

Artie backed away, hugging Bluey to his chest.

'It won't cost me nuffink at the Blue Cross.'

But the man was determined in this at least and because Artie wouldn't take the money he left it on top of the garden wall. Then he went back to his car and drove off. When he had gone, Artie put the money in his pocket. There was no sense in leaving it there for someone else. Then he crossed the road and went back to the wooden bench beneath the chestnut tree, where he had promised to wait for Jeff.

*

It seemed as though Jeff would never come and despair filled the whole of Artie's thin body while he waited. Bluey wasn't dead, that was certain. She wouldn't remain so limp and yielding if the car had killed her. At the same time, she must be badly hurt or she wouldn't stay so still and lifeless.

He hardly dared move her, with the vague knowledge that it might be harmful to do so, and while he sat so still for so long, passing his hand constantly along her as if love alone could restore her to her former vigour, every kind of thought possessed him, each one more depressing than its predecessor.

He didn't cry now. Tears weren't going to help Bluey get better, but every time his imagination repeated the terrible picture of her being tossed into the air, a shudder went right through him, covering him all over with goose pimples.

At last he saw Jeff, who waved and broke into a half run at the sight of him. He couldn't run very well – it was a

lopsided gait which he soon abandoned – but he had
guessed that something was wrong. There was that about
Artie's lonely figure which struck him with anxiety.

He didn't say anything after Artie explained what had
happened. He just sat beside him on the bench, looking at
the cat, scratching behind his ear, which was his custom
when something troubled him. They both watched a man
pass by with a big black-and-tan Alsatian. He looked at
them, saw the cat, but kept on walking, bending to pick
up a stick to throw to the dog.

'What did Mum say?' said Artie at last, fondling Bluey's
ears while he spoke.

'Nuffink. She wasn't there. I looked around in the
kitchen and on the sideboard to see if I could find the
address written down somewhere, but she must've got it in
'er purse.'

Artie made no comment so, after a pause, he went on.
'What we going to do then?'

'We'll 'ave to take Bluey down to the Blue Cross. 'Ave
we still got enough money for the bus?' He had completely
forgotten about the pound note in his pocket.

Jeff pulled out five new pence. Artie clicked his tongue
and sighed.

'We spent the rest on the bus,' Jeff reminded him. 'This
is what I got left over from yesterday.'

'You'd better keep it then to go 'ome wiv. I'll go down
there by myself.'

'But you can't walk all that way with the cat. It's in
Tooting, isn't it?'

Artie nodded. 'I'll put 'im in the bag just in case 'e
wakes up on the way.'

Carefully he laid her in the bag, recalling as he did so
the force and energy with which she had escaped the
cardboard box half a dozen times hardly more than an

hour ago, and he bit his lip to push away the pain of remembering.

The walk to the Blue Cross Dispensary took him almost an hour and he was tired and dispirited by the time he got there. The vet, Mr Fielding, knew him well because Artie had been there several times, leaving an indelible memory of his cheerful talkative self.

The first time he had gone with a blackbird, rescued from the school cat in the playground. The teacher had told him about the Blue Cross and the whole class took an interest in the bird's fate. Mr Fielding kept it for a week and, when it was fully recovered, Artie took it to the nearest park and let it fly away. Then he discovered a fledgling, fallen from its nest. It was ugly, with bulging black eyes, huge beak, featherless except for a few bristles on the wing-tips. Mr Fielding said he would try to feed it but it died.

Another time Artie went to see him bursting with indignation because of a dog which was kept tied up in someone's back yard, and yet again when his pet mouse died, hoping somehow that Mr Fielding could bring it back to life, before Jeff finally buried it.

When he walked into the consulting room, his pale face thinner still with its expression of tiredness and dread, Mr Fielding immediately knew that something was wrong.

'Goodness me, Artie!' he tried to rouse him. 'What is the matter?'

Artie confined himself to an explanation of the accident alone, using surprisingly few words, and Mr Fielding listened attentively, as he always did, because he was a man dedicated to animals and infinitely patient with those who cared about them even if they did sometimes waste his time.

'Let's have a look at him then,' he said. 'Where've you

got him? In this bag? Get him out, then. We'll see what we can do.'

Much to Artie's surprise, Bluey was conscious when he opened the bag. She looked as though she had just woken from a heavy sleep and stared with bewilderment as he took hold of her.

'Ah well, at least she's conscious,' began Mr Fielding cheerfully, but he shook his head and sighed when Artie put her on the table.

He didn't need to say anything. Artie could see what was wrong. Bluey couldn't stand up. Her hind legs were completely useless.

Tears welled in Artie's eyes but he blinked them away. Bluey didn't seem to feel any pain so there was still hope. Again he blinked away the persistent tears, twitching his nose with emotion.

'Oh dear me, Artie,' said Mr Fielding. The tone of his voice was sufficient, without any further explanation.

'Can't you get 'im better?' he asked, forcing his restricted throat to behave itself.

Mr Fielding smoothed his hands over the cat's hindquarters. Bluey turned her head to look at him but otherwise didn't move. He lifted her up and squeezed her back with his fingers and Artie expected her to yowl with pain.

'All the feeling's gone,' commented Mr Fielding. And he pummelled her harder to prove his point.

'What's the matter with 'im then?' begged Artie, his voice hardly more than a squeak. 'Can't you do *somefink*?'

He shook his head.

'Not when it's a broken pelvis. If it were just the legs, I could plaster them up. But it's the whole back. The bones are so delicate. Probably they're all smashed to pieces. She's not in any pain, as you can see. The nerves are quite paralysed.'

'Then 'e'll be all right? I mean, if 'e's not in pain . . . '

'It's best to have her put down, Artie. She can't walk any more. She can't run or jump. She can only drag herself about. It would be unkind to keep her.'

Artie was silent, letting the words sink in. Bluey couldn't die. He loved her. She belonged to him. Besides, she was only young. You could see she was hardly more than a kitten. She couldn't die just because of that split-second collision with a car. His thoughts were interrupted by Mr Fielding's next words.

'You needn't worry. She won't feel anything. I'll give her an injection and she'll just go off to sleep.'

'No!' cried Artie, rousing himself. 'You can't do that. You can't kill 'im. Not if 'e isn't in any pain.'

'But, Artie, be reasonable.'

'Cor!' he exclaimed bitterly. 'Suppose they'd said the same about my bruver. "'E can only drag 'imself about so you'd better 'ave 'im put down". 'Ow do you know if 'e'll be un'appy? My bruver's 'appy enough and 'e's only got one leg and it 'urts 'im sometimes too. If Bluey's not even going to 'urt . . . '

'But it's different for a cat,' Mr Fielding broke in. 'You can't compare your brother with——'

'Why not? Bluey's alive, isn't 'e? 'E's got feelings, 'asn't 'e? And I love 'im like if 'e was my bruver.'

Mr Fielding examined Artie closely. He was quivering all over, his thin face scarlet with emotion, tight with indignation. He could remember himself as a boy, defending a sick animal with greater devotion just because it was sick and needing him more, and all his sympathy was with Artie. He had been blunt, he had told him the truth, but it hadn't frightened him. If anything, it made him love the cat more, and who was he to deny Artie's

belief in his ability to keep the cat happy in spite of its
incurable injury?

'Well, I can't force you to have her put down,' he
admitted, 'but it'll be hard work looking after her. You'll
have to do everything for her. Keep her clean, make sure
she doesn't get tangled up in anything, watch her the
whole time. Are you prepared to do that and, more
important still, are your parents prepared to keep a helpless cat in the house?'

Mr Fielding didn't know much about Artie's family but
he could guess from the boy's appearance and from
previous conversations that he was pretty well independent, making out as he could with little parental super-
vision or even care.

'Is she really your cat?' he asked. 'She's a Russian Blue,
you know. Where did you get her?'

' 'E was given to me,' he lied, suddenly afraid that
Mr Fielding might be empowered to take her away from
him.

'Who by, I wonder? There's not many people who'd
give away a Russian Blue.'

'It was a friend of my Mum's. She couldn't keep 'im.'

'Well,' said Mr Fielding, not convinced but aware that
stranger things happened every day, 'look after her as best
you can and if you need any advice come and see me. If she
seems to be in any distress, or pain, bring her at once,
won't you. You'll promise me that?'

Artie nodded.

'I won't forget. You needn't worry, Mr Fielding. 'E'll
be all right wiv me. I'll look after 'im, you can be sure
of that.'

7. Abby

When Artie got home only Jeff was in, waiting for him. The younger ones were playing down in one of the court-yards, enjoying the evening sunshine in their swimsuits, and no one ever knew where the older ones got to. Mr Shaw had gone to the pub, as usual, and their mother wouldn't be back from Bingo until nearly midnight. Artie was relieved.

Carefully he took Bluey out of the bag and put her on his bed. She was no longer frightened, the events of the last few hours having bewildered her so much that there was no room for fear. From the expression in her wide-apart eyes, Artie could tell that she was still a bit dazed. Both boys began to stroke her and when Artie wriggled his fingers she pricked her ears, though making no attempt to catch them as was usually her custom.

' 'E's going to be all right,' said Artie confidently.

'But what did the vet say?' Jeff wanted to know and, before Artie had finished telling him, exclaimed, 'But you can't keep 'im. Mum won't let you. She'll be mad enough when she finds you 'aven't taken 'im back to that woman. And when she sees what's 'appened . . . Cor! I'm glad I'm not going to be in your shoes.'

'Well, I'm going to keep 'im. I don't care what Mum says,' insisted Artie stubbornly. 'You'll 'ave to 'elp me.'

'I think you're nuts!' said Jeff, looking at his brother with exasperation.

'Aren't you going to 'elp me then?' demanded Artie fiercely, his face red and glistening in the hot airless room.

'I don't know. I still say Mum won't let you 'ave 'im.'

Jeff was quite right. When their mother discovered the cat's presence the next morning she was furious. She didn't want to hear Jeff's explanations or Artie's excuses and, until she had delivered a couple of blows to Artie's head and finished shouting about their stupidity and disobedience, she didn't even realize that Bluey was crippled. When she did understand, she was even more furious.

'You won't get no fiver now,' she shouted. 'I don't suppose the woman'll even want 'im.'

'Then let me keep 'im, Mum. Let me keep 'im. 'E won't be no bovver. Honest. 'E can't tear up no more curtains, or fings like that. 'E'll just stay in 'is box till I come 'ome to look after 'im.'

'That's what you think! Take 'im back. I'm not 'aving sick cats dragging themselves round 'ere. Bad enough with all you lot as it is,' and Artie pleaded in vain.

She told him to take the cat back directly after breakfast. As it was the last week of school she didn't care much whether he attended the last few classes or not. It wasn't as if he was going to learn anything.

'But what shall I do if the woman don't want 'im?' said Artie. 'I can't just leave 'im in the street, can I?'

'You leave 'im with the woman. It's 'er cat and it's 'er responsibility. If she won't 'ave 'im, you take 'im down to the Blue Cross and 'ave 'im put to sleep, but don't come back 'ere with 'im or I'll stick 'im in a bucket of water myself, I will.'

Artie didn't believe she would really carry out her threat but, while she was in that mood, it was no good trying to reason with her. He knew she didn't like sick animals, or even scratchy dogs, so it was useless to plead any longer. If he brought Bluey back, she wouldn't drown her, but she would be capable of taking her down to the vet to have her put to sleep.

He found an old jersey in which to wrap Bluey. He wasn't going to put her in the bag again, especially as she couldn't escape, and hugging her closely in his arms, he walked heavily down the stairs. He walked all the way to the common, Bluey's ears quivering at the noise of the traffic and all the different street sounds. She dug her claws into his arm, not meaning to hurt him, just expressing her anxiety, and Artie could feel her trembling against his body.

He talked softly to her all the while so that she wouldn't be too frightened, lifting her head closer to his own and crooning the words into her pricked ears. Her fur tickled his nose and made him want to sneeze. It was more like fur than hair because it was so thick. Artie had never known a cat with such a plush, dense coat. Everything about Bluey was different to other cats, her colour, her coat, her sharp ears, her vivid green eyes, her affectionate ways, and he couldn't bear the thought of having to part with her.

As he grew closer to the common, he began to think about Bluey's owner. What would she say when she saw her condition? More important, what would she do? Suppose she decided to have her put to sleep? Mr Fielding spoke as if it were the only remedy, even though she was so valuable. He wondered if Mrs Bradley would think the same way or would she feel, as he did, that Bluey had a right to live even though she was crippled?

He reached the place where Bluey had been run over the day before and stopped. No, he just couldn't take her back to Mrs Bradley. He couldn't take the risk. He went over to the chestnut tree on the corner of the common and sat on the bench beneath it. He unwrapped the jersey from Bluey's body and put her on the ground, no longer afraid that she would run away but curious to see what she would

do. She looked up at him, her almond-shaped eyes
expressively questioning.

'What's the matter, Bluey?' he said softly, leaning down
to stroke her. 'You'll 'ave to get used to it, you know. It'll
be all right when you're used to it.'

She clung to his fingers with oval-shaped paws, turning
onto her back and squirming in the sunshine. As long as
he was close to her she didn't seem to mind about being
half-paralysed, she didn't seem to notice, but the minute
he left her to herself she became timid and unsure.

He knelt down beside her, tickling her chest, grinning
with pleasure as she tugged again at his fingers. 'You're
all right, aren't you, Bluey? You're all right wiv me.'

There was no one on the common at that time of the
morning. All the children were in school and the people
who took their dogs for walks were doing other things.
Blackbirds were pecking at the grass and Bluey watched
them, her ears taut. She was still lying on her back and it
made Artie laugh to see the way she stretched her head
back as far as it would go to watch them.

He wondered if she saw them upside down and got
down beside her in the same position to find out. They
weren't really, not if you twisted your head slightly, the
same as she did. Of course, she couldn't twitch her tail like
she used to, nor lope after them, but she watched them
steadfastly, with the sun shining through the leaves in
dappled patches on her blue-silvery underparts.

She was just as alert, just as keen, as if she were able to
run after them, and Artie twitched his nose indignantly as
he recalled Mr Fielding's words. And Mrs Bradley wasn't
having her. Oh no! She was bound to feel the same way.
Grown-ups always did think the same way about everything. They were used to doing what everyone else did
and if you asked them why, and why you couldn't do it

some other way, their only answer was, 'Because that's the way it is, that's why.' Probably they didn't even know why, otherwise they'd think of a better answer.

But if he didn't take Bluey back to Mrs Bradley, what was he going to do with her? He couldn't take her back home and he didn't know anyone who could look after her for him. It was all very well deciding to keep her, but how was he going to do it?

*

Artie was still lying in the grass beside Bluey, trying to look at things upside down and finding this view of the branches far above his head a novel one, when he was aware of a pair of brown, white-socked legs close beside him. He jumped up quickly, reddening with confusion, and found the owner of them, a thin, coloured girl at least a head taller than himself, grinning at him with obvious amusement.

'Sorry,' she said, meeting his distrustful stare with an even wider grin. 'I didn't mean to disturb you. I just wondered what you were doing.'

Artie didn't think much of girls as a species but he was used to them, because of his sisters, and besides, this particular girl had a way of smiling that disarmed all suspicion.

'It's all right,' he said gruffly. 'I was just looking at the trees.' It seemed a poor sort of answer so he added, 'They look different upside down.'

To his surprise, she threw her satchel on the ground and a second later was stretched out beneath the tree, looking up and shading her eyes from the sun which glinted on her glasses.

'You're right,' she agreed. 'They are different.' After a short silence, she went on, 'I can see a bird's nest. Did you see it?' She pointed. 'On that branch to the right. Nearly at the top. I wonder if there's any birds in it?'

Then she got up and dusted the bits of twigs and grass from her dark green gymslip. She looked at Bluey who was watching her suspiciously, half pressed to the ground as if ready to resist her advances.

'Is that your cat? Isn't she lovely!'

''Ow do you know 'e's a she?' asked Artie in surprise. He himself was always forgetting.

'Because she looks like a girl. Can't you see what a sweet, narrow face she's got? Tom cats have got rounder faces. Hadn't you noticed?'

He shook his head.

'What's wrong with her?' she went on. 'Can I touch her? Will she mind?'

'I don't know,' said Artie. ''E mightn't if you don't frighten 'im.'

The girl knelt down, some distance away from the cat, and called to her softly, stretching out a slender brown hand, close enough for Bluey to sniff at if she wanted to but not close enough to be menacing. Artie could see that she understood animals and his respect for her grew.

'E got run over yesterday,' he said, forgetting that he didn't even know the girl's name or that he'd only met her a few minutes before.

Bluey was cautiously examining the tips of the girl's fingers, stretching forward to do so, and soon she was allowing the stranger to fondle her ears and rub her under the chin, purring with pleasure. Meanwhile Artie poured out the whole of Bluey's history during the last five days.

'You did right,' she affirmed with a nod of her head. 'I wouldn't have let the vet put her to sleep either.'

By now Bluey was on her lap, kneading her claws into the green gymslip, rubbing her muzzle up and down the sleeve of the white blouse, still purring like a machine. And Artie wasn't even jealous, although he had allowed no one but Jeff to touch her until now.

''E likes you,' he said.

'She,' she corrected. 'Don't keep calling her "him". All animals like me. I bet I could even make friends with a tiger.'

''Ave you got any pets?' he asked, sitting on the grass beside her and helping her to make a fuss of Bluey.

'No. My Mum's allergic to animals so I can't have any.'

'Allergic!'

'Yes. You know, like hay fever, only it's animals that affect her instead of hay. She's only to get near a dog, or even a toy animal made of rabbit's fur, and she goes all spotty and her face swells up, so I can't have any animals. I've got some goldfish, but that's all.'

She began to laugh, a high-pitched, infectious sound which made Artie want to laugh too. Then she sobered and asked, 'What's your name?'

'Artie.'

'Mine's Abigail.' She pulled a face and went on hurriedly, 'Everyone calls me Abby. I reckon my Mum looked my name up in one of those baby books and didn't have time to get past the first page.' Again she laughed. 'It's a horrible name, isn't it?'

Artie shrugged. 'I've never 'eard of it before. But Abby sounds all right.'

Abby was even more talkative than Artie and she had no prejudice whatsoever about making conversation with a boy nearly two years younger than herself. Everything she said was punctuated with the same, hearty laughter which seemed to be constantly bubbling inside her, glistening in her dark eyes. Bluey fell asleep on her lap, wooed by the sun and her gentle hands.

Abby went to a grammar school in Battersea. She had only recently moved into a small flat in a converted house near the common and so far knew no one in the neighbourhood. She had no brothers or sisters and lived alone with her mother who worked for a dental surgeon.

'Does she pull out teeth?' Artie wanted to know.

'No,' she laughed. 'She couldn't even pull out mine when they were loose. She's hopeless. She was learning to be a dentist before she had me, but then she had to go to work. Now she's a secretary.'

'What about your Dad?'

'Oh, I think he was a student, too, only he went back to Africa and Mum didn't want to go there. She can't stand the heat, so just imagine if she went there!'

'I'd like to go to Africa, exploring the jungle . . . '

'I think it's all explored by now,' she interrupted. 'But you could be a game warden, or something like that.' She looked at her wristwatch. 'I ought to go. I've got to get back to school in time for lunch. We're breaking up tomorrow. What about you?'

'Not till Friday. But I don't know if I'm going back this week. Not if I 'ave to look after Bluey, I'm not. If I leave 'im – 'er – with my Mum she's bound to take 'im – 'er – down to the Blue Cross and then she's done for.'

'We'll have to think of something,' agreed Abby, and for once her expression was serious as she looked down at the sleeping cat and smoothed her hand over the deadened hindquarters. 'Listen,' she went on. 'I really must go now but I'll be back by about five o'clock. If you could be up here then, I'll come and look for you. I might have thought of something by then. What do you think?'

Artie nodded. 'All right. I'll be 'ere.'

She put Bluey in his arms, picked up her satchel then with a quick wave was off, running down the road with long, easy strides. After she had gone it seemed to Artie that her laughter was still ringing in his ears.

8. The shed

Abby kept her promise. She was already on the common, sitting on the bench beneath the chestnut tree, when Artie arrived and greeted him, 'You're late. I thought you weren't coming. It's gone half past five already.'

'Sorry,' said Artie. 'I 'aven't got a watch like you 'ave so I didn't know what time it was, did I?'

He was only too glad to hand Bluey over to Abby for a while. His sun-reddened face glistened with perspiration and his arms ached as if they'd been stretched on the rack, as in a film he'd recently seen on the television. Bluey mewed protestingly but soon quietened down when Abby bent her brown face over her and began to talk coaxingly.

'You're a darling,' she said softly. 'I wish you were mine,' and she murmured a lot of other things in a similar vein.

Artie interrupted her. 'Well, did you fink of somefink?'

She nodded. 'I had an idea this afternoon. There's an old shed in our back garden. Used to be for gardening tools and things like that. When we first moved in my Mum asked Mr Bennett – that's the owner of the house – if I could use it as a den, and he said all right if I didn't mind cleaning it out first. I started but it's in such a mess that I didn't get very far. But if you like to help me, we could get it clean enough for keeping Bluey there and, being nearby, I could keep an eye on her for you.'

It sounded the perfect place to Artie and when he actually saw it he was quite convinced. Abby took him through the house, along a passage well decorated and softly carpeted which led to the back door and the little-used garden beyond. There was a small, overgrown lawn, with gooseberry and lavender bushes encroaching upon it, and a tangle of red and white roses clambering over the high black fences. In one corner, in the shade of a neglected apple tree, was the shed, its glass windows cracked and cobwebbed, some of its boards loose or buckled.

'We could buy a padlock,' said Abby as she opened the shaky door, 'although no one ever comes here. Mr Bennett said I must want my brains tested if I wanted to play in this place.' Here she again exploded with the laughter that was an essential part of her character.

'It's super!' said Artie, although he could hardly distinguish anything in the gloomy interior, adding to its attraction for him. 'Cor! I wish I 'ad a place like this. You aren't 'alf lucky.'

'Wait a minute. I've got a candle here somewhere. There's a shelf. . . . Here we are.'

The matches were damp and Abby struck several before managing to light the candle. The pupils of Bluey's eyes narrowed in the sudden glare.

'It's a wooden floor, so it's not bad really. We could find a bit of old carpet. The second-hand furniture man sells rugs for about ten pence,' went on Abby enthusiastically.

Artie was speechless with delight. When Abby had stuck the candle in an old jam jar to keep it from toppling over, he left Bluey in her arms and explored the shed from end to end. It was about six feet long, lined with shelves that were as much covered with cobwebs as old paint tins and rubbish. At the far end there was a work bench which had been cleared.

'We could throw out all the old tins and things,' said Abby, 'and clean the windows and put up some curtains. My Mum's got lots of bits left over from where we lived before. We could make it like a real little room and Bluey would soon feel at home here.'

Artie grinned and twitched his nose with pleasure, Abby's words conjuring up all sorts of comforts and delights.

'Are you sure it'll be all right? I mean, what about the neighbours. Don't they come out 'ere?'

'I don't think so. Mr Bennett's got rheumatics or something so he doesn't bother with the garden any more, and no one else has the time anyway. They're all out at work all day.'

'What about kids?'

'I'm the only one. Mr Bennett doesn't like children, but he said I could stay because I'm almost grown up, and I'm quiet.' She almost doubled up with a screech at this, covering her mouth with her hands, delighted at Mr Bennett's mistaken idea of her.

'Where we going to put Bluey then?' said Artie after a while. 'Where's she going to be most comfy?'

Abby looked thoughtful.

'Under the bench, in the corner,' she said decisively. 'We could put a box for her on top of some of these old planks so she's not on the floor in the draughts, and perhaps later we can put an old curtain across the bench for when it gets colder.'

Abby laid Bluey out on the lawn in the shadow of the apple tree, leaving her to preen her foreparts and bite at the long grasses while she and Artie got to work inside the shed. While Artie piled all the rubbish in one corner, Abby went back to the house for a bucket of water and some rags for cleaning the windows. She also brought a broom for the cobwebs, which Artie tackled, because spiders made Abby shiver, bringing most of them down on his head.

Abby laughed delightedly. 'If you could see yourself!' she exclaimed. 'You'd better have a wash in our kitchen before you go home.'

'I don't want to be no bovver,' he said, and then another thought occurred to him. ''Ow am I going to come and see Bluey on my own? I mean, I can't just walk in and out as I fancy, can I?'

'There's the back gate, in the other corner. You can use that. We've got a key.'

'And what if Mr Bennett sees me 'ere?'

'You tell him you're a friend and you're waiting for me. But his rooms look out over the front so it's not likely that he'll see you.'

'What about your Mum? She might see me.'

'Yes, but she won't mind. I expect I'll have to tell her about you and Bluey anyway. But she's all right, is my Mum. She won't make a fuss. She lets me do as I like as long as it's reasonable. She says I'm sensible.'

It was growing dark by the time the little shed was as tidy as they could make it. Abby had brought an old suitcase from the house for Bluey to sleep in and she tied the lid to a nail in the bench to keep it from falling down on the cat's head. She had also brought a cushion from her bed, an old rag doll, two chipped saucers, one of which she filled with water while Artie tipped the crushed remains of the fish dinner he had bought at mid-day into the other.

Abby had to go indoors to have her supper and Artie sat beneath the apple tree with Bluey beside him, stroking her gently under the chin, and feeling suddenly alone. All the time Abby had been with him, he had overflowed with optimism but now, in the gathering darkness, he was beginning to wonder how Bluey would feel about being left to herself in the strange shed.

Bluey flicked her ears as the gnats whined round her but Artie didn't even notice them. He wished he could stay all night with her, sleeping under the tree because the air was fresher outside and it wouldn't be so dark with the starlight, and he considered leaving Bluey in the garden instead of in the shed. But suppose it rained? You could never tell. Even the best days could turn to rain, very often did, and she wouldn't be able to move herself out of the wet. No, she would have to go in the suitcase, but he sighed heavily, for the first time niggled by doubt.

*

When Artie got home it was very late. He suddenly realized that he was hungry but his mother had nothing to offer him except a chunk of bread and jam and some cornflakes.

'If you can't come 'ome at a reasonable time you can't expect nothing,' she told him crossly. 'Where you been all this time anyway?'

'I took the cat back, didn't I?'

'That was this morning. What you been doing since then?'

'Just messing around. I didn't feel like coming 'ome.'

'And what did the woman say?'

For a moment Artie didn't answer. He hadn't thought of preparing an explanation but by the time his mother repeated the question he was confident enough to tackle it.

'Cor! She wasn't 'alf mad at first. But I told 'er it wasn't my fault that Bluey got out of the bag and in the end she calmed down.'

'Did she give you anything?'

'A pound. She said she couldn't give me no more 'cos 'e wasn't worf it now.'

'You're not lying to me I hope, Artie Shaw,' said his mother, staring intently into the sweaty, freckled, dust-grimed face. He opened his pale eyes wider.

'I spent some of it 'cos I was 'ungry. Went to the chip

shop.' He pulled some coins out of his pocket. ''Ere's the change.'

Mrs Shaw sniffed deprecatingly. 'You'd better keep it. Do as pocket money for the summer 'olidays. No point in putting that in the post office.'

Then she seemed to tire of the subject, leaving him to eat his bread and jam in bed with Jeff beside him to ask him what had really happened.

'Promise you won't tell if I tell you?'

'Course I won't.'

'Say, "On me muvver's death-bed".'

'On me muvver's death-bed.'

'Say, "See it wet, see it dry, cut my froat if I tell a lie".'

Jeff repeated the jingle, licking and drying his finger and miming the slitting of his throat as was required by the oath, but still Artie eyed him uncertainly.

'Come on,' urged Jeff. 'When did I ever tell on you? We're mates, aren't we?'

'Is Dave asleep?'

'Dead,' assured Jeff. 'You know 'e never wakes up once 'e's off.'

So at last Artie told him of the day's adventures and when he finished Jeff exclaimed, 'Wow! You don't 'alf get yourself into some scrapes. Suppose someone finds out? Suppose that woman still wants 'er cat back?'

''Ow's she going to find 'im, that's what I'd like to know? 'Ow's she going to find 'im? Only if someone tells 'er. And who'e going to tell 'er?' His tone was belligerent.

Jeff shrugged his shoulders. 'It's your funeral, mate, if anyone finds out.'

'They can't do nuffink. I 'aven't done nuffink wrong.'

'No,' retorted Jeff sarcastically. 'Only keeping a cat that doesn't belong to you, and telling lies, and bovvering people. That's all.'

'Oh shut up. It's not you as is going to get into trouble, is it? It's not you as 'as to take the blame.'

And Artie threw himself back on the pillow, overcome with tiredness and not wanting to argue any more. Jeff's practical instinct was depressing. He needed encouragement, perhaps because instinctively he realized that his undertaking to keep Bluey was going to be harder than he pretended, and just now he was too tired to feel optimistic. Even the recurring memory of Abby's bubbling laughter no longer cheered him. It seemed almost mocking, as he remembered it in the moonlit room, feeling so tired but unable to sleep.

Jeff had gone back to his own bed and was now asleep with his mouth open, an elbow sticking through the torn pyjama sleeve, and Dave was snoring slightly in the bunk-bed above him. Everyone else must be asleep too because the telly was switched off and no one was talking or making any kind of noise. There wasn't even a light shining under the door.

Unthinkingly, he stretched out an arm to touch Bluey who had slept curled up by his knees for the last four nights, and pain suddenly swelled in his heart when his fingers touched the empty blanket. It had been so comfy, having Bluey on his bed, licking his fingers with her rough, hard tongue, purring in the darkness. What was she doing now, on her own in that old, black shed? Was the moon shining through the cracked window which Abby had washed that afternoon? Was she awake, like he was, feeling lonely and afraid?

He shook his head impatiently to dash away the tears that trickled down his nose, and wished and wished that some kind of magic could change the happenings of yesterday, so that everything could be as it was before.

9. Mrs Bradley

Mrs Bradley despaired of Sacha's homecoming. She had waited expectantly on the Monday evening from five o'clock onwards, growing impatient by half-past, worried by six o'clock and definitely annoyed by seven. At eight she was quite sure that she wouldn't see Sacha that day but was not made any happier by her correct assumption.

On Tuesday she felt more hopeful, having thought of various explanations for Sacha's non-appearance the previous evening, and she spent the whole day indoors, certain that someone would bring back her Russian Blue.

When Wednesday and Thursday had gone by she was in an agony of doubt, impatience and despair. What had happened to Sacha? Why hadn't she been returned as the phone caller had promised? Had something terrible happened to her cat or had the finder changed her mind about parting with her?

Mrs Bradley was nearly sixty, a grey-haired widow with no children who had dedicated her affection and her lonely lifetime to poodles and dachshunds and sharp little Cairn terriers. The last dog had died more than a year before she bought Sacha. She felt herself too old now to start again with a puppy, which needed so much patience and attention while small, and had decided to breed Russian Blues as a lucrative hobby.

She had had to wait a year for Sacha, because Russian Blues were in short supply, and the green-eyed, slinky, sinuous kitten had cost her a lot of money. Her parents, her grandparents, her great-grandparents were all champions and Sacha had only been sold to Mrs Bradley as a special favour, because she was on friendly terms with the woman who bred her.

'If you don't want to show her, you must at least breed from her,' Mrs Bradley's friend had insisted. 'Otherwise I can't possibly let you have her. There's so few like her in the country that it's a pity to waste her just as a pet.'

So Mrs Bradley had promised, feeling rather proud of her Sacha and very serious about her undertaking. Sacha was the perfect companion for her, apart from being an exquisite example of her breed, her dark blue coat and emerald eyes filling her with pride and drawing the attention of all who saw her.

Sacha had made herself at home in the quiet, unflustered way of Russian Blues, rarely voicing either complaints or pleasures, except in a soft purr deep in her throat, and loving nothing better than to stretch herself out in Mrs Bradley's lap, either to sleep with her head hanging down, or to preen her lustrous hair.

The months went by and Mrs Bradley guarded her zealously, not even letting her lie out in the garden unless she was there to watch her. She didn't expect Sacha to be stolen but she was afraid that one day she might wander off and get lost or, worse still, run out into the road beyond the garden and perhaps be killed. While Sacha was a kitten she accustomed her to wearing an elastic collar with a little bell, to which she attached a lead, and when she didn't have time to watch Sacha in the garden she would fasten the lead to a stake in the lawn and know that she could safely leave her.

While she was very small Sacha didn't mind the lead. She played with it and filled it with teeth- and claw-marks. But as she grew older she liked it less and less. The birds in the trees, the whispering leaves, the blackbird that sung on the chimney pot, were a constant torment to her, and she tangled herself so often and grew so distressed that Mrs Bradley had to give up tethering her.

But she kept the elastic collar and Sacha had to suffer the indignity of wearing it while she was out. It was taken off indoors, in order not to spoil the shape of the hair round her neck, but while she was in the garden she had to carry her address round her neck. Otherwise Mrs Bradley was afraid to let her out, even though she was watching her all the time.

So how did Sacha run away? How did she get lost?

It was one of those things that happen so quickly. Sacha was in the garden, pouncing about in the pile of weeds which Mrs Bradley had been arduously removing from her marigold border, when the postman opened the gate to bring a small parcel. Almost immediately behind the postman, a large mongrel was passing. He happened to spy the cat, dashed in with a volley of blood-curdling barks, and Sacha flung herself through the privet hedge into the road.

For a second she was caught there, struggling with the collar which had caught in a branch, but the dog's closeness and the threatening sounds exploding from him, the cries of Mrs Bradley and the shouts of the postman terrified her into violent motion. She dragged her head free of the collar and fled along the road, disappearing abruptly down a side street before Mrs Bradley could look for her.

Only a minute or so had passed between the dog's arrival and the cat's disappearance but neither Mrs Bradley, nor the postman who obligingly helped her, could discover Sacha in the nearby gardens. For days Mrs Bradley searched for her, wandering for hours over the common, looking up into every tree, enquiring of all her neighbours, trekking round every back street and alley, getting permission to look into garages and garden sheds, but Sacha had completely disappeared.

Until she received the phone call six days later she was utterly distraught and, when the days went by after she had been promised the cat's return, her distress was only exceeded by her annoyance and the growing conviction that whoever had found her Russian Blue had decided to keep her.

Eventually she went to the police. She went a week after the phone call, on a wet Monday morning that didn't seem to belong to summer at all, so miserable and cold was it.

The policeman at the duty desk carefully copied down Sacha's description in a big register but Mrs Bradley wasn't content to leave it at that. She explained about the phone call and the reward she had offered and went on, 'I'm sure that whoever it was that phoned me was made to realize the cat's actual value and either decided to keep her, or even to sell her for a greater price than the reward.'

'How much is this cat worth then?' the policeman asked.

'Some people would be prepared to pay thirty pounds or more. She cost me twenty-five guineas as a kitten so you can see I'm not making a fuss about nothing. Quite apart from the fact that I'm fond of her, she's a rare and valuable animal, and I must have her back.'

'Well, Madam, I don't quite see what we can do. If you actually knew who's got her. . . . Pity you didn't think of asking for the lady's address when she phoned you. We can circulate a general description. Someone might have seen her, but if someone is keeping her because she's valuable, it's hardly likely that they're going to have her on show, is it?'

'There must be something you can do,' insisted Mrs Bradley desperately. 'I must have her back. It's imperative.'

'Why not try advertising again? And if anyone does ring you the next time, get their address or their name at least.'

Mrs Bradley snorted scornfully. 'I can't see that advertising will help now.'

'Have you tried the local vets? They might know something. It might be worthwhile getting in touch with them. Or get on to the breeders of Russian Blues. Find out if anyone has been offered a cat like yours.'

'Suppose I discover her whereabouts,' asked Mrs Bradley thoughtfully. 'Suppose someone's got her and they won't give her up?'

'In that case you ought to come and see me again. Stealing by finding. We certainly could do something about that.'

With this Mrs Bradley had to be satisfied. Someone else had come in and was waiting to talk to the policeman, so she went out into the rain again, pushing up her umbrella determinedly. At least she had something to do and she would find her Sacha, no matter how long it took her.

*

When she reached home, Mrs Bradley put the kettle on to make herself a cup of tea. Even this action reminded her of Sacha, who always came running to welcome her if she had been out, tail stiff in the air, rubbing her head against Mrs Bradley's legs while she prepared the tea things. Sharply she shook herself free of thoughts and her feeling of loss and, while the tea was settling in the pot, went for the telephone guide and turned to the Yellow Pages.

She set out a notebook and fountain pen then, while she

sipped the hot tea and nibbled a shortcake biscuit, she noted down the names and telephone numbers of all the veterinary surgeons listed there from as wide a circle as Barnes and Richmond to Kensington and Fulham. She also found a list of breeders of Russian Blues and noted down any London telephone numbers, deciding she would write to the rest that afternoon. When she had done all this she sat back in her chair to think, letting her mind ponder over the telephone call, wondering what could possibly have happened to Sacha since then.

During the next few days Mrs Bradley contacted all the vets on her list. She wrote dozens of letters and waited impatiently for the replies, having enclosed stamped

addressed envelopes regardless of expense. She advertised in the national newspapers, both daily and evening editions, and wrote out half a dozen postcards to stick in the local shop windows.

Keeping herself busy in this way, she was newly filled with hope and didn't have time to feel her loss so greatly. She was surprised to discover how much she missed Sacha for, having been a breeder of dogs for so many years, she had always rather scorned cats, declaring that they couldn't possibly be so much company as dogs, being selfish, haughty and independent.

But now that Sacha was gone, she recalled how the sandpaper tongue would gently lick her fingers of an evening, while they listened to the radio together. She recalled the soft, oval-shaped paws, that touched her cheek with delicate gentleness, and the rhythmic, contented purring that lulled her to sleep every night while Sacha shared her bed. An independent soul herself, Mrs Bradley had learned to appreciate Sacha's lack of humility and she would never again call a cat selfish after Sacha's daily example of pleasure in her company.

The days went by and from everywhere came the same answer. No. No. No. She renewed the postcards in the windows, she contacted homes for stray and unwanted animals, she even got in touch with the R.S.P.C.A. but no one could help her with her enquiries.

The lady in the little corner grocery shop, in whom she had confided most of her daily toils and pleasures for many years, said to her one morning, 'I don't like to see you getting into such a state, my dear. Isn't it about time you forgot that cat and gave up spending so much money looking for her? If you haven't heard anything by now, it's very doubtful that you will get any news.'

'But I can't give up trying. I can't. Somehow I have a

feeling that I'll find her. I can't explain it. I just have this feeling.'

'Why don't you have one of my little puppies? I know they're not pedigrees or anything like that, but they are sweet, and their mother's the loveliest dog I've ever come across. I know you've never had dealings with mongrels before but they're good company and just as intelligent as any thoroughbred, if you don't mind my saying so.'

'I can't start again with puppies. They're such hard work, the first six months or so, and I'm not so young as I used to be. They're so dirty and they need such a lot of exercise——'

'You've got that big garden.'

'It's not enough. He'd dig up all the flowers and I've just got it looking nice, after years of bones and holes.'

'You've got the common in front of you.'

'Yes, but I can't walk like I used to.'

'It's a pity,' sighed the shop-keeper. 'I'd rather you had one of my puppies than anyone. Think about it. They're only five weeks old, so there's plenty of time for you to change your mind. I'll save you the prettiest, just in case. . . .'

'It's very kind of you, but——'

'If you don't get your Sacha back, you just come and ask me for one of my pups. You'll never regret it, that I'm sure.'

Mrs Bradley went home feeling unusually down-hearted. Perhaps the shop-keeper's confidence that she wouldn't be successful in her search had undermined her at last. She thought of the newspaper bills she had to pay. At least fifteen pounds they added up to. Sacha wasn't worth so much, not now. . . . But she would have given fifty to have her Russian Blue once more. And she laughed ironically to herself at the thought. That's what loneliness and old age had brought her to. Fifty pounds for a cat!

She put on the kettle for her usual morning tea, then the phone rang. Her heart leaped as it always did these days, but it drooped just as suddenly. It was probably a wrong number. She sighed as she went to answer.

'Who is it? Mr Fielding? The Blue Cross. Where did you say?'

And all of a sudden she could hardly understand what the voice at the other end of the line was telling her. A casual glance at an old evening newspaper . . . a Russian Blue cat, female, brought to his clinic at least a fortnight or three weeks ago . . . injured, badly injured, but still alive.

'Just a moment, just a moment, please!' she cried, overcome by the varying emotions of joy, disbelief, fear and hope.

She took several deep breaths, counted up to ten and then asked Mr Fielding to repeat his story. When he had finished she gratefully promised to send a donation for his collecting box, then she made a fresh pot of tea because she really needed it.

By the time she had drunk it down, hot and sweet, she had ordered the thoughts that were spinning in her head and was carefully considering Mr Fielding's information. A boy called Artie, undoubtedly the son of the woman who had phoned her; and a place called 'The Fairbright' of which neither she nor Mr Fielding knew the location, except that it must be somewhere reasonably near to Tooting. It shouldn't be too difficult to find the latter and then a few careful enquiries would sort out the identity of freckle-faced, poorly dressed Artie.

Artie! Mrs Bradley's thoughts lingered over the unknown child whose carelessness had caused Sacha's accident and yet whose devotion had prevented Mr

Fielding destroying her. He had been warm in his description of the boy and assured her that the cat was in affectionate hands at least.

But mostly her thoughts were with Sacha. Her lovely Russian Blue helplessly crippled and being cared for by an ignorant boy who probably didn't have the slightest idea of her needs. It was all very well to love her, but love wasn't enough in a case like this. She wondered what she would have done under the circumstances, had she been the person confronted with Mr Fielding's advice, and what she would do when she got Sacha back.

She just didn't know. She did admit to herself that she might well have agreed with Mr Fielding. A smashed pelvis, a body half paralysed! Was it fair to oblige any animal to drag itself about in that condition. Could any animal possibly be happy? Wouldn't it be kinder, as he had said, to have her destroyed?

At any other time she would have come to the answer easily, but Artie's adamant insistence on life at any price made her wonder if there might be something in favour of his primitive reasoning. Perhaps a child, who was closer to nature, who was still unaffected by the accepted norms of the adult world, could be nearer in understanding to the animal mind.

Once she had Sacha in her arms again she could find out. She would listen to Artie's explanations, see if he could convince her, if not with words at least with Sacha's appearance after so many days of helplessness. If he couldn't convince her, if she saw Sacha ill and unhappy. . . .

Oh, she couldn't bear to think any further. To have Sacha so near, after so much anxiety, but to have her thus. . . . It was too cruel.

10. In the garden

Meanwhile, Artie had no doubts himself as to the Russian Blue's happiness. He had none of Mrs Bradley's sentimentality, because there had been little sentiment in his life so far. He had only his love, the love of a generous heart, which made him determined to keep Bluey as contented and comfortable as possible, and his uncomplicated confidence in Bluey's fondness for life in spite of her crippled state.

He didn't try to pretend that she would get better. Mr Fielding had told him it was impossible, but Artie had long ago learned to live with reality at the time of his brother's accident. From small boys onwards, when they had shared the same bed, he and Jeff had been inseparable and when Jeff was lying dangerously ill in hospital, and the doctors still weren't sure if they could save his life, let alone his mangled leg, Artie had been the one to stay with him instead of their mother.

Jeff, in his delirium or moments of wakefulness, hadn't cried for his mother. He had cried only for Artie until, after much doubt and argument, the doctors had placed a cot for Artie beside his own so that they could be together constantly.

For days that grew into weeks Artie had lived at the hospital, cheering his brother with his perky chatterings and matter-of-fact confidence in Jeff's recovery, and the harrowing experience became such an ordinary part of their daily lives that soon it meant almost nothing to them, except in terms of physical pain which Jeff would have had to fight alone had not Artie been there to grin and make fun of everything.

Both Jeff and Artie had more or less forgotten those days, nearly five years ago, half a lifetime, but they served Artie now in his practical attitude towards Bluey's disability. The pain that had been the worst part of Jeff's experience, was non-existent for Bluey, and therefore Artie had no doubt whatsoever that she must be glad to be still alive.

She greeted him with a mew of delight when he arrived at the garden each morning, even though she might be in Abby's arms at the time, and began to purr as soon as she felt his hands about her ears and throat. She would press her teeth gently into his hand and stroke him with her oval paws, while her pricked, pointed ears seemed to listen to every word he uttered.

Bluey was hardly ever alone. Abby was always there when Artie wasn't and often she brought her lunch and her tea down to the garden when he had to go away for his own. Even though he didn't say so out loud, Artie had to admit to himself that only Abby made it possible for him to keep the cat. She nursed Bluey with the gentlest of care. She had brought rags in large quantities from a jumble sale at the church hall, with which to keep Bluey as clean as possible and took pleasure in the attentions the half-paralysed cat needed.

She seemed to know quite a bit about nursing and things of that sort and it was her idea to give Bluey's hindquarters a careful massage twice a day.

'What for?' Artie wanted to know, watching the long brown fingers knead the feelingless parts in knowledgeable fashion.

'To keep the circulation going. I read it in a book once. It helps to keep the muscles in good condition.'

'But she can't use 'em, anyway, so what difference does it make?'

'It might make a difference. You never know. We ought to try everything, at least, to keep her in good condition.'

It was also Abby's idea to make her mobile by attaching her to a light, wheeled platform which she could drag along by the efforts of her forequarters. This idea had come to her after watching Bluey's attempts to get about, reminding her of a legless man she had once seen pushing himself along the street on a low sort of trolley.

They both quickly discovered that Bluey had no intention of remaining completely stationary, especially as her strength and self-confidence grew with the passing days. Last thing every night, Artie would tuck her comfortably into the suitcase under the workbench and first thing every morning he or Abby would find her stretched out by the doorway, waiting to be let out.

They watched her drag herself across the untidy lawn, tangling herself in the long grass stems and waiting patiently for them to come and release her when her own efforts were insufficient, and tried in vain to keep her to the comparatively easy footpath which ran from the shed to the back door of the house.

Bluey was determined to explore wherever fancy took her, even if by the time she had reached her destination the thing that had attracted her had vanished. She watched the gooseberry bushes with narrowed eyes and quivering ears, sometimes licking her jaws when the jerky movements of the sparrows and blackbirds taunted her beyond endurance. Her claws dug in the ground, her whiskers twitched as if with small electric shocks, and her eyes seemed to glow with excitement and anticipation.

'She's so beautiful!' Abby would exclaim, tirelessly watching her.

Perhaps it was because she was a girl that Abby worried so much about appearances. She had a soft brush which had belonged to someone's baby, three pence at the jumble sale, with which she was always smoothing Bluey's dense coat. An unnecessary process really, Artie thought, because its very density kept it tidy. She would take off her glasses in the garden, even though she couldn't see very well without them and look at herself in a hand-mirror, another jumble sale acquisition.

'Do you think I'm getting lighter?' she would ask Artie from time to time. 'My Mum says so. She says by the time I'm grown up I should look Spanish or Italian, or perhaps Greek.'

'Well, you look the same to me,' said Artie.

He might have got a bit fed up with her, going on about her looks, if she hadn't had such good ideas. Bluey's 'wheel-chair' was the best one. She drew a sketch of her idea and immediately Artie set about finding the pieces for it.

He took the six rubber wheels off Jason's brand new fire-engine. They were about four inches in diameter, solid, and just the size required. Jason bawled like anything when he found his sabotaged toy but no one seemed to know anything about the missing pieces and in the end he got the blame for breaking it.

Between them they sorted out a flat piece of wood from among the jumble in the shed and Abby carefully glued a bit of felt on top of it to make it comfortable. The most difficult part was fixing the wheels but Artie was determined when he started on something and after a couple of days the cart was mobile. The next difficulty was trying to convince Bluey that nothing terrible would happen if she allowed herself to be attached to it.

Getting the feelingless hindquarters comfortably settled was easy, as was tying the tapes across Bluey's back. But the tape that went round her chest annoyed her exceedingly and she tugged and chewed and grew wildly angry at being subjected to such indignity.

'She doesn't 'alf make fings difficult sometimes,' sighed Artie, scratching his head and twitching his nose. 'Now what do we do?'

Abby frowned thoughtfully, then laughed and said, 'Just wait for her to get used to it.'

And that's how it was. After fighting in vain to remove the tape, and sleeping with it for a couple of hours, Bluey decided that it was harmless after all. The most comical part was when she discovered her unusual mobility. At first she was startled, unable to understand it, and she kept looking round, a very worried frown creasing her slanting forehead.

Abby rolled in the grass with laughter, exaggerated in all her ways as usual, and this was just as startling for Bluey. She almost forgot about the little cart, watching the girl, and when she moved again the same surprise, the same bewilderment brought the same screeches of laughter from Abby.

Within a few days Bluey accustomed herself to the 'wheel-chair' and was learning the advantages of it. Sometimes the wheels got tangled in the grass, until Abby decided that the grass must be cut. Artie spent a whole back-breaking day with a pair of rusty garden scissors, snipping at daisies, weeds and resistant tufts. Abby borrowed her mother's kitchen scissors and between them they cleared a large circle round about the shed and apple tree, where she most liked to move about and where it was least likely that she would be seen from the house.

So far Bluey's existence in the garden was undiscovered. Abby's mother knew about her and insisted that Abby wear a special overall which she removed before returning to the house. She was also pretty obliging with odd bits of material, spare cups and other odds and ends which made the shed more comfortable. She hadn't met Artie, either because she hadn't time or wasn't interested, but Abby assured him that she had no intention of interfering with either of them as long as Mr Bennett made no complaints.

One day Abby said, 'That woman's still looking for Bluey. I saw an advertisement in the newsagents. "Reward for information leading to the recovery of a valuable Russian Blue cat". She must live fairly near here. I hope she doesn't discover her one day.'

'Not if we never take 'er out of the garden, she won't, and what we want to do that for?'

Artie had considered taking Bluey about with him before this, because sometimes he tired of the garden and of Abby's exclusive company. Jeff had come there on two or three occasions but it was too far for Jeff to make it very often unless they had money for the bus fare. Apart from that, Jeff was a bit of a nuisance. He kept on about Bluey being discovered one day, and the trouble Artie would get into, and Artie was fed up with listening to him. Jeff was far too cautious for his liking.

Jeff spent most of his day at the Play Centre, at which the whole family was entitled to free dinners during the summer holidays, and he liked being there because he had the run of the school library and could bury his nose in books all day long. Artie only went for his meal then came running back to Bluey. He was supposed to stay there all day, as if he were at school, but his mother didn't really care where he went so long as he kept out of her way. She usually gave him ten pence to make sure that he wouldn't need to come home to ask for something.

Keeping Bluey supplied with food was no problem. Abby, who was reading books about cats at the library, mixed her a small portion of breakfast cereal each morning and in the afternoon chopped up a plateful of liver or rabbit pieces which Bluey accepted with her usual delicacy and obvious satisfaction. She wasn't a big eater so what with Abby's pocket money and Artie's and Jeff's odd shillings combined (because Jeff didn't need to spend his while he was reading in the school library) Bluey never went hungry.

Artie would have been perfectly happy, had it not been for the realization that Mrs Bradley was still looking for Bluey. He had just about forgotten that Bluey had ever belonged to anyone else and that there had ever been a time when she didn't belong to him.

Abby said, 'Perhaps she loves Bluey just as much as we do. After all, wouldn't you keep on looking for her if you'd lost her?'

Artie reluctantly agreed. 'I suppose so, but you'd fink she'd 'ave got tired by now, wouldn't you? I mean, she could've bought 'erself anovver one, couldn't she? She must 'ave lots of money if she keeps on about rewards, mustn't she?'

'If it wasn't a Russian Blue, maybe she wouldn't mind so much. In the book I read it says they're very scarce and difficult to come by. Perhaps that's why she wants her back.'

Abby had told Artie all the things she read about cats and now he knew almost as much as she did. Now he knew why Bluey was so different to other cats with her foreign-looking appearance, strange colouring and emerald eyes. She was Russian. If she'd been anything else, an ordinary, everyday cat, Artie would have been a lot happier. Now he knew she was valuable he couldn't help worrying. In a way, it was like stealing, keeping Bluey when he knew Mrs Bradley wanted her back so badly, but he couldn't help believing that Bluey was only safe in this deserted, forgotten garden.

*

Sometimes the sun shone, sometimes it rained. The gooseberries grew ripe among the leaves and branches and Artie ate most of them, giving himself a very bad feeling one day. There were tiny apples budding among the leaves of the apple tree but most of them shrivelled up without growing very big. Wasps and bees buzzed about, collecting pollen from the wilderness of neglected marigolds, forget-me-nots, and the ivory roses which clambered from the next-door-neighbour's fence.

On rainy days Abby brought cards and taught Artie to play Rummy. They laughed more than they played because Artie was hopeless at concentrating or sitting still very long. He'd rather be out in the garden, even if it was raining.

One day Abby said glumly, 'Isn't it a swindle? Next week I've got to go away on holiday.'

Artie didn't think it was a swindle at all. He still had very agreeable memories of his two weeks in the country.

'Where you going?' he asked.

'It's a little village down in Kent, where my grandparents live. They've got a cottage. It's lovely really, and they're all right, I suppose. But I hate leaving Bluey now she's getting so fond of me.'

Artie privately thought it wouldn't be a bad idea for Abby to go away for a while as Bluey did indeed seem to be very fond of her. Although he wasn't jealous by nature – who could be jealous with the rough-and-ready family upbringing that he was used to? – there was a niggardly feeling inside him when he watched Bluey rub her head against the brown cheek, purring with deep contentment. He wanted Bluey to love him and no one else.

Before she went away, Abby wrote her grandparents' address on a piece of paper. 'Don't lose it,' she said. 'I'll stick it in this tin up on the shelf. Will you remember?'

'I don't suppose I'll be writing you any letters,' said Artie.

'No, but you never know. My Mum always leaves an address if we're going away somewhere. She says it's wise.' She sighed and stroked Bluey's head. 'I wish I could take you with me, darling.' To Artie she said, 'My Gran likes cats. She's got three, big, fat things. They're not half as sweet as Bluey. Terribly spoilt and selfish. If one day we couldn't keep Bluey I'm sure she'd have her.'

Abby went away and Artie began to miss her. The garden which had resounded with her constant laughter was strangely silent. Even Bluey noticed her absence. She went round the lawn on her trolley, mewing plaintively. Bluey hardly ever mewed so Artie knew it must be that she was calling Abby. He untied her from the cart and held her close in his arms, burying his nose into her chest. She caught him round the ears with her paws, only just digging her claws into the flesh, but very gently, and her sandpaper tongue licked the side of his head.

'You're mine, mine,' he told her. 'And I'll never let you go.'

A few evenings later, when he went home, his mother was waiting for him and by the look on her face he could see that something was up. Her lips were pursed tight, making her cheeks look fatter than ever, and her eyes bored right through him.

''Ere you, Artie Shaw,' she called as he tried to slink past her to his bedroom, 'just come 'ere a minute. I want to 'ave a talk with you.'

Artie stopped but he didn't get too close. She was frying sausages and usually the smell made his mouth water.

D

But not this time. His mouth had gone all dry and he thought his heart would stop beating. Somehow, without knowing why, he was sure it had to do with the cat.

'That Mrs Bradley was 'ere today. You know who I mean, don't you?' and when he shook his head without looking at her, 'The woman whose cat you found.'

A breathless pain caught in his stomach and he licked his lips nervously.

'She still 'asn't got 'er cat. You told me you'd taken it to her. Why did you tell me a lie? Why did you say you'd taken it back and tell me all that rigmarole about 'ow cross she was and so on? Who's got the cat anyway, and where did you get that money from, the pound she was supposed to 'ave given you? Come on, Artie boy, out with it. I've 'ad enough lies from you and I'm not 'aving any more.'

11. Betrayal

Artie's mind raced. He had to think of some good answers, quick, or she would never believe him.

'Well, come on,' she repeated. 'Out with it. I don't want none of your lies. This time I want the truth.'

She towered over him, hands on hips, forgetting about the sausages spluttering and bursting in the frying pan.

'I was going to take 'er back. Really I was. . . . ' What could he say? What could he say? Come on. Think of something. 'I was taking 'er back, honest, but – but she wasn't in. She must've been out shopping or somefink. I kept ringing and ringing . . . '

His mind was beginning to work now. He knew something would come out of it if she let him talk long enough. She turned to look at the sausages at last and this small break was all he needed to gather his wits.

'So I went on the common to wait for 'er. And while I was there this woman come by.'

'What woman?'

'I don't know who she was. But she got talking to me, asking about Blu – about the cat and all that, and she said she was fond of animals and knew 'ow to look after 'em and if I liked she'd buy 'er off me. And she give me the pound.'

'And what about Mrs Bradley? What about all them lies you told me?'

'I was scared of taking 'er back to Mrs Bradley. I fought she was going to be angry wiv me and all that, so I give 'er to this other woman.'

'And Mrs Bradley was going to give you a fiver. Why did you let 'er go for a pound?'

''Cos I fought, I bet that Mrs Bradley won't give me nuffink now, she'll be so mad.'

His mother looked at him, her mouth tight with anger and disbelief. Artie's eyes flickered to her hands, wondering if she would let fly with one of them and not knowing which it might be. She was equally agile with either and, although she didn't often hit anybody, once she got going she was a whirlwind of furious blows.

'Artie Shaw, if you're telling me any more lies I swear I'll clean you so as you'll never forget it as long as you live.'

Inwardly he shook, because he knew she might.

'Mrs Bradley's coming again tomorrow. She wants that cat and is determined to 'ave it. I'm going to look a right Charley when I tell 'er what you've just told me. And if it ain't true . . . '

'It's true, Mum. It's true. I give 'er to this woman on the common. I did, honest I did.'

'Go on, get out of 'ere,' she suddenly shouted at him, and Artie gladly escaped, right out of the flat rather than just to his room where he would still be within reach. 'Bloomin' kids,' he heard her say as he slipped out of the door. 'More trouble than they're worth.'

He went back to the garden and hugged Bluey in his arms. She was so docile she didn't mind how much she was picked up and fussed, never struggling away from him, never scratching, except sometimes in play. His heart was thumping and his face burned. He'd run hard most of the way and, apart from this, he was filled with anxiety.

That Mrs Bradley was after him, he was sure of that. Somehow or another she'd find out that the story about the woman on the common wasn't true and then she'd be bothering his mother again, keeping on an on until

the truth was out. He was afraid. She'd take Bluey away
from him. She wouldn't care about how much he loved
her. She'd take her away and perhaps have her put to
sleep.

It was a warm evening. Artie wasn't feeling hungry now so he didn't want to go home. He leaned against the trunk of the apple tree with Bluey across his knees, purring until she fell asleep and was silent. Gnats were dancing about. He could hear crockery clattering nearby, where he supposed a neighbour was getting supper ready for someone. A dog was barking, a baby was crying, and two men were carrying on a conversation in slow voices.

It was so peaceful in that garden, with the unkempt flowers growing in spite of the weeds, and the grass so green in the last of the sunlight, and Bluey's fur coat gleaming in patches where the sun touched on it, that Artie felt as though he never wanted to go home any more.

He remembered what Abby had told him about Russian Blues, something she had read in a book at the library. The Russians had believed they had the power to keep away the evil eye and everyone liked to have one in their home, or even just a picture of one, to put in their babies' cradles to protect them in the night. He wished he could take Bluey home and let her sleep with him. He wished he could stay here with her and that her special powers would keep Mrs Bradley from ever finding out about this quiet garden.

Could there be any magic in her? Artie normally scoffed at such rubbish. Fairies and all that sort of thing were for babies. But there was something about her, something strange that had attracted him in the first place and made him love her so much. Was it in the snaky shape of her body, the weird greenness of her slanting eyes, the exaggerated sharpness of her ears? There was something witch-like in her appearance, something magic in the colour of her coat, that in his fears and longings, Artie could almost bring himself to believe the Russian folk-tale.

The sky grew dark. There was a glow across the lawn
from the back windows of the house. It was time to put
Bluey in her bed and go home.

*

Artie kept out of his mother's way for the next few days.
This normally wasn't difficult but she seemed to stay at
home more often now, no doubt waiting for him because
Jeff told him that Mrs Bradley had been again and was
very cross at the news their mother had given her.

'Why don't you give 'er up?' Jeff begged him again.
'She doesn't seem a bad sort really. Perhaps she'll look
after Bluey all right.'

Artie just shook his head dumbly. He didn't have any
reasons now. He just intended to keep her.

Jeff went off to the Play Centre as usual. It was at a
school near home and he was happy there, reading all day
long. He and Artie sat together at lunch-time but, apart
from this, they hardly saw each other at all. Artie came
home at night later and later, staying with Bluey always
until the last moment, and Jeff was often asleep before he
came in.

Jeff was at home when the policeman called with Mrs
Bradley and because he knew more about Artie's goings-
on than anyone he came in for all the cross-questioning.
Between them all they asked him half-a-dozen times about
the woman on the common, what Artie did with his spare
time, where he went, who were his friends, where was he
now. The policeman said that if Artie still had the cat and
refused to return it, then it would be stealing and he could
get into serious trouble.

It was amazing how quickly the rumour ran all round
the flats that a policeman had called on the Shaw family
and that one of them was in trouble. At the gates of the

courtyard a crowd had gathered to watch him leave.

Jeff was worried sick. His never very robust features were paler than usual and he couldn't eat his supper, sitting silent and thoughtful while everyone else made a noise and Mrs Shaw insulted the police force in general and Mrs Bradley in particular. In the end she turned on the silent Jeff and shouted, 'If you know anything about that brother of yours, you'd better own up. That is, if you don't want to see 'im in a Remand 'Ome this side of Christmas.'

Jeff burst out, 'All right. All right. 'E's still got the cat. I don't know where 'e keeps it, but 'e's got it somewhere. I'll tell 'im 'e's got to bring it 'ome.'

'I'll tell 'im,' said Mrs Shaw, swelling with rage. 'Just wait till 'e comes 'ome.'

'Don't 'it 'im, Mum. Please don't 'it 'im. It's only 'cos 'e can't keep an animal 'ere. 'E didn't mean no 'arm.'

'No 'arm! With all the lies 'e's told me. If 'e don't bring that cat back 'ere this very night I'll knock 'im silly, I swear I will. I'm not 'aving no more of 'is nonsense. Taking the mickey out of me. 'Aving the police round 'ere. I'll learn 'im.'

Artie didn't come home although the hours went by. Mrs Shaw stayed in although she was supposed to be at the Bingo Club. She was in a terrible temper because it was a special night, that night, with the big prize up to two hundred and fifty pounds and she was hoping to win it. Mr Shaw had waved his hands and shut his ears. He'd heard enough of that cat already and as soon as his supper was swallowed he'd gone off to the pub.

Jeff crept out when his mother wasn't looking. He had to wait twenty minutes for the bus that would take him as far as the common, choked with anxiety and not even sure that he would find Artie in the garden. Suppose he was on

the way home, walking, while he passed him in the bus?
He looked out at the abandoned, darkening streets but
saw no one. The bus went too quickly, its bright lights
leaving all outer things in a shadow, and he wouldn't
have recognized Artie had he been there.

By the time he reached Abby's garden, going up the
back lane as Artie had shown him, almost an hour had
gone by. He banged on the shabby green gate, with the
peeling paint.

'Art! Art' It's me. Jeff. Open up. Quick.'

An age passed before Artie opened the door. Bluey was
in his arms, looking as startled as Artie.

'What's up, mate? What's 'appened?'

'A policeman's been round 'ome and Mum's going mad.
Says she's going to kill you if you don't come back wiv
that cat.'

''Ow she know I've still got it?' snapped Artie accus-
ingly, his eyes gazing narrowly into Jeff's. 'Who told 'er?
Who let on?'

'They said you'd be 'ad up for stealing. They said you'd
be put in a Remand 'Ome and I fought——'

'You told on me, didn't you? You promised you
wouldn't tell. You swore. You said——'

'But, Art, I 'ad to tell. What would you 'ave done?'

'I'd 'ave kept me mouf shut, like I promised, that's
what I would've done. You're a rotten, stinking big-mouf,
that's what you are, Jeff Shaw, and you're not my mate
any more.'

The two boys stared at each other, Artie's face drawn
with bitterness, Jeff's stunned with disbelief.

'I only wanted to——'

'Shut up and get out of 'ere. They didn't 'ave to know.
If you'd 'ave kept your trap shut. . . . They couldn't prove
anyfink. You're just a big-mouf, that's what you are. You

didn't want me to keep Bluey, anyway. All along you've been on at me about getting rid of 'er and now you're bloomin' well glad, aren't you? Aren't you?'

'It's not true. I . . . '

'Well, just you listen to me, mate.' Artie wouldn't let him finish, or even defend himself. 'You'd better not tell where I got Bluey or I'll make you wish you'd never been born, just see if I don't.'

He turned sharply away, muttering to himself. 'Now what am I going to do?' then looked back with a harsh glance at Jeff, who still stood there, illuminated by the house lights, a crushed, sorry figure but for whom Artie felt no pity at all.

'What you still standing there for? 'Aven't you done enough already? Get back 'ome and do a bit more sneaking. But you'll never be my mate no more.' His voice was choked with indignation.

Jeff went away without another word and Artie slammed the gate behind him and pushed home the bolt. He went into the shed with Bluey and put her on the work bench which Abby had cleared and covered with an old checkered table cloth. There were flowers in a jampot, wilting because they'd been there far too long. On the wall behind the bench Abby had pinned lots of pictures of animals, cats mostly. But there wasn't a Russian Blue among them. The nearest thing to Bluey was a Persian of similar colouring. It had amber eyes and its hair was too long but Artie had called it Bluey anyway.

He stared at the pictures and Bluey stared at them too. At least, she seemed to be staring at them until he saw the spider ambling across the tabby's nose and knocked it down for her. He watched her mangle it up with the paws that were so soft against his cheek and felt a bitter satisfaction when she'd finished. He felt like mangling something too. He wanted to hit and kick and punch.

Until now he had never felt the bitterness of betrayal and it was a hard, bursting pain which crushed his chest and bored right through his stomach. How could he? How could he? How could he? If he couldn't trust Jeff, he couldn't trust anyone.

He thumped his clenched fists on the table. The jar and the flowers bounced and Bluey looked up with startled expression.

What would Jeff do now? Would he tell where the garden was? Would he bring Mrs Bradley or the police to the garden gate, just as he had come himself a short while ago?

He'd have to find a new place for Bluey. He didn't dare keep her here any longer. What about tonight? Would she be safe for tonight? Surely no one would come for her right now? By the time Jeff got back it would be too late for anything. He hoped he'd have a good long wait for the bus. Better still, that he wouldn't have any more money and would have to walk home.

A momentary pang shot through him for the meanness of his thought, then the remembrance of the betrayal surged through him again and any compassion for his brother was vanquished.

After a while the fit of pain and anger passed. He sat under the tree and tried to think but he was either too tired or too overwrought to make sense of the plans and half-plans that came and went. It was time to go home but how could he go home with his mother waiting to belt him and Jeff in the bed beside his own, converted into a traitor?

He would stay in the shed and sleep with Bluey. Perhaps tomorrow he'd be able to think more clearly. Tomorrow morning early he would find a new home for

Bluey and he'd never tell Jeff a word about it, not Jeff
or even Abby when she came back. He wasn't going to
trust anyone any more.

There was a new feeling in his stomach now, one of
hunger. He suddenly remembered that he'd had no tea
or supper and that if he didn't go home he wouldn't get
any. He delved his hands into his pockets but produced
only two pence, not enough for anything except a stick
of liquorice or a tube of peppermints, and the kind of
hunger he felt wouldn't be satisfied with that.

There were some dog chocolate drops in a tin on one
of the shelves. Abby had bought them for Bluey, in case
she might like them, but although Bluey liked bread and
jam she didn't take to the chocolate drops. Artie found
them and after he had experimentally chewed a bit of the
first one, decided they tasted like any other chocolate
drops and ate the whole tinful.

He felt a bit sick when he'd finished and pulled a few
gooseberries off the bushes to take the sweet taste out of his
mouth. He was terribly thirsty but there was nothing he
could do about that unless he drank Bluey's water, which
he didn't fancy, and the bottle in which he'd brought it
from home was empty.

He went to the shed to decide where he ought to sleep.
There wasn't really much room on the floor because
Abby had bought a chair and a table which took up most
of the space. They were made of cane and Artie thought
he might be able to curl up inside the chair and sleep
quite comfortably. He tried it for a while but was soon all
cramped up and stiff.

There was a blue rug which Abby had bought at the
second-hand shop for twenty-five pence, patchy in places
but soft underfoot. When Artie lay down on it, intending to
sleep there, it didn't seem so soft. He kept twisting and

turning but there was no denying it. The floor was very hard and there was a nasty draught too.

Bluey watched him curiously from her suitcase, long ears pricked. She couldn't understand what he was up to.

In the end, as it looked as though it wouldn't rain, for there were no clouds and every star was glittering, Artie took both Bluey and the rug outside. He pulled his anorak over his shoulders and felt about as comfortable as he was likely to feel. The best part was having Bluey curled up beside him.

She was very pleased to share his company, dragging herself as close as she could. She pushed her muzzle into Artie's arm-pit and, sucking at a bit of his T-shirt, which she had caught between her teeth, began kneading his ribs with her soft paws until she had nursed herself to sleep.

Artie didn't move, although he felt a bit wet and uncomfortable. But he didn't want Bluey to stop. He stroked her with a free hand and a lump swelled in his throat as he thought of that Mrs Bradley getting her back. The only thing he had ever had to call his own, the only thing he really wanted!

His mind wandered on to Jeff. He still couldn't understand how his brother could have betrayed him – so easily too. He would never have sneaked on Jeff. They would have had to tear him apart before they got any secret out of him. Fancy! His brother Jeff, ratting on him as if it didn't matter at all.

He couldn't sleep. The ground was hard and cold, in spite of the rug. The night air was damp and there were all sorts of sounds which jerked him into wakefulness as he was drifting off; mice-like scrambles, the sharp hoot of a car, the constant movement of the leaves of the apple tree. Only Bluey didn't move. She, at least, was fast asleep.

What was he going to do with Bluey? He couldn't just leave her anywhere. And what would happen now that Jeff had told everyone that he still had the cat? He'd have to give her up. What with Mrs Bradley and the police, they'd never let him keep her.

Tears of helplessness welled in his eyes and his heart was crushed with despair. She'd kill her, he knew she would. She wouldn't want to keep a crippled cat. Mrs Bradley, his mother, Jeff, the police, Abby . . . they all went through his mind again and again, like a roundabout that couldn't stop but whose revolutions led absolutely nowhere, always back to the same place.

A terrible hate, a wild feeling of revolt filled him. People were always wanting to order him about while not caring anything about him. His mother was waiting to beat him, perhaps his father too. The police would accuse him of stealing. Mrs Bradley would blame him for Bluey's accident and Jeff. . . . He could hardly bear to think of Jeff.

Why should he go home? Why shouldn't he run away with Bluey? Why should he have to go back? They'd be sorry if they couldn't find him. They'd wish they hadn't been so mean. They might even miss him a bit.

A grim smile came with these thoughts. He'd show them. He didn't know what he'd show them, but he didn't care. He was hurt and wanted to hurt, and whatever happened he wasn't going to let anyone kill Bluey.

When he fell asleep it was almost dawn and the moonlight was beading the dew on the flowers and bushes and lawn.

12. Pursuit

Artie woke with a start. At first he couldn't make out where he was and wondered if he were still dreaming. The sky above his head was solid grey and he couldn't even guess what time it was. Bluey was awake, a puzzled expression in her green eyes, and then Artie remembered everything in a rush. With remembrance came a feeling of stiffness and cold. He had tossed off the anorak in the night and the only warm bit was where Bluey still lodged against him.

With a half groan, half sigh, he sat up, rubbed his eyes and scratched his head. He had been dreaming and his dream was still more real to him than anything else.

There had been cats everywhere, but mainly the big tabby of the picture stuck on the wall in the shed. He had gone to Abby's grandparents with Bluey, full of hope, but when her grandmother opened the front door at his ring, a whole load of cats came pouring out, cats of every colour and size, but dominated by the tabby who took an instant dislike to Bluey.

'I can't possibly have Bluey too,' exclaimed Abby's grandmother. 'There's just no more room and even Charley (Artie instantly knew that this was the tabby) says the same. He's eaten three cats already so I couldn't possibly take any chances, you see,' and she laughed just like Abby, only somehow it was converted into a horrible, hysterical sound which sent shivers down Artie's spine even now, while he was wide awake.

But in the dream Abby persuaded her grandmother to keep Bluey and, as Artie went away down the front garden path, he heard the Russian Blue shrieking. Looking round, he saw her clawing at the front window with Charley close beside her, almost converted into a tiger, dragging at her with his claws. And the horrible thing was that Bluey couldn't escape him because she was paralysed.

A shiver ran down Artie's back as he went over the dream involuntarily, and he screwed up his eyes to shut it from his memory. He got up from the rug, after stroking Bluey for a moment or two, and stretched his arms and legs. His spirits were at their lowest. He wished Abby were there to cheer him up. She could have given him some breakfast too. Hunger was overpowering him now but he was determined not to go home.

He remembered that Abby had left fifty pence in the old paint tin to help towards the cost of Bluey's food while she was away. Abby always seemed to have plenty of money and she was generous with it. Artie thought about the money and the ethics of using it for purposes other than those set out by Abby. Normally he would never have touched it, except for Bluey's cereal or the rabbit pieces at the butchers, but perhaps the occasion could be called exceptional. After all, if he hadn't gone home it was because he was protecting Bluey and if he bought some breakfast at the tea-shop it would be for the same reason.

Thinking this way, and struggling with his conscience for at least ten minutes, until his stomach hurt so much that he couldn't think any longer, he reached up for the tin and the fifty-pence piece. There was the envelope with Abby's holiday address on it. He put the money inside it, folded it up and pushed it in his trouser pocket.

He was going to leave Bluey in the garden but changed his mind. Suppose Jeff turned up while he was gone, perhaps with Mrs Bradley or a policeman? No, he wasn't taking his eyes off Bluey not even for a minute, not now he wasn't. So he put on his anorak, zipped it up halfway, then pushed Bluey inside. She was comfortable there and quite happy, having grown used to being carried about like this. She poked out her head and her ears quivered excitedly as Artie went down the back lane and into the street.

He went in a different direction this morning and to judge by the few people about imagined it must still be early. When he reached a shopping parade all the shops were still shut and a clock in a newsagent's, the only place open, said it was ten past seven. He passed a block of flats and a big used-car lot, then on the other side of the road saw a café which was open.

There were two men in a corner seat eating egg and chips so he ordered a plateful for himself and had a cup of tea to be going on with. Bluey stretched her head out of the anorak as far as she could, looking with wondering, curious eyes at her surroundings.

'What a pretty cat!' exclaimed the woman as she slapped down his breakfast. 'Wouldn't have thought you'd want to bring it out in the street. It might jump out and get run over.'

'No. She's used to being carried,' he said and then he attacked the egg and chips, his hands almost trembling as they held the knife and fork, so hungry was he. The food disappeared in next to no time and he was still feeling empty.

'Can I 'ave anovver lot?' he asked.

'If you can pay for 'em, have as many as you like.'

The second plateful he ate more slowly, cleaning it round with bread and butter and giving a few bits to Bluey. She liked the chips soaked with egg yolk as much as he did and ate three. By this time he had put her on the chair beside him because it was difficult to eat with Bluey's nose almost poking into his mouth with every forkful.

There was only twenty-two pence change from the fifty by the time he'd had a second cup of tea and when he left the café, feeling fuller and more cheerful, it had begun to rain. Bluey flicked her ears every time a raindrop hit them.

Artie hurried back to the garden. He remembered he'd left the rug out on the grass and Abby would be cross if he let it get ruined by the rain. When he got back there, approaching cautiously just in case someone had arrived before him, he suddenly realized what he must do. It was really the only thing he could do. He couldn't keep Bluey hidden in different places, hoping she'd never be found, because sooner or later she would be and, besides, winter would be coming and she couldn't stay out in the cold.

In spite of his dream, he'd take her down to Abby's grandparents. She said her grandmother loved cats and he knew she wouldn't refuse to have Bluey. Abby would persuade her, anyway. She was very persuasive, and Mrs Bradley would never find her there. He tried to remember what Abby had said about the place. She had gone on her own, from Waterloo Station, and it was two stops before Gravesend. When you got off the train you had to take the local bus which stopped right outside her grandmother's cottage.

The only trouble was he didn't have much money left, at least not enough to get right down into Kent. He thought of Jeff, who would be on his way to the Play Centre at about ten o'clock. He could hang around outside the Fairbright for him and ask him to get some money from home. But how could he trust Jeff any more?

He'd already betrayed him once. He twitched his nose, bit his lips, and made up his mind. He'd have to take the chance.

Artie wasn't in luck. The first persons he saw before he'd even got near to the Fairbright were his brothers, Phil and Brian, on the opposite side of the road. Even as he dodged into a shop doorway, they saw him and let out a shout.

'Come 'ere, you little——' but Artie had already broken into a run in the opposite direction before Phil could finish. ''Ere, Bri, catch 'im before 'e gets away. 'E's got that cat wiv 'im too.'

Artie had the advantage in that his brothers couldn't get across the road because of the traffic, which was now constant and rapid. Even so, they weren't far behind him and could run faster than he could. He didn't stop to look back but raced with panic-stricken heart, wondering where he could hide before they caught up with him and dragged him triumphantly back home.

He didn't know where he was running to. He didn't have time to look. All he was aware of were the shouts of his two brothers above the noise of the rush-hour traffic. They had crossed the road now and were about a hundred yards behind him. He went up a side street and round another turning, flashing past the stables where the rag-and-bone men kept their ponies, almost tripping over a cat which dashed out from under a cart.

'What's all the rush about, mate?' a cloth-capped fellow asked him in amazement, side-stepping a head-on collision, but Artie had no time for explanations. Phil and Brian were still fairly close on his heels.

The railings of the Wandle were just ahead, with a bridge that crossed into the park. Suddenly he remembered the gap in the railings on the other side of the bridge, down by the big plane tree. If he could get down there before they saw him. . . .

Throat choked and painful, heart almost bursting, he slithered through the gap and down the bank, feeling a thousand pricklings start in his legs as he went through a patch of stinging nettles right in his path. His breath came in sobs as he staggered lopsided along the bank, pushing Bluey back into his anorak, for she was frightened now and struggling to get out. He tried to say something to her to calm her, but the only sound he was capable of uttering was the gasp of his tortured lungs.

He looked towards the bridge. Phil and Brian were standing on it, looking the other way. In a minute, when they couldn't see him, they'd come over to this side. If he could get behind those bushes near the railings perhaps they and the tree trunks might block him from their sight.

Tall, weedy white flowers grew up the bank, together with clumps of dandelions and thick grass. Artie's strength was failing and the rain made the bank very slippery. At last he reached the bushes, which were thick and thorny and cruelly uninviting, but in spite of the jabs and scratches they gave him, Artie crept almost gratefully among them and stopped at last to catch his breath.

He could still see his brothers although they couldn't see him. He couldn't hear what they were saying but they were looking in his direction and then Brian pointed. Phil shook his head but Brian insisted and in a minute they were crossing the bridge, no doubt looking for a way onto the bank. They'd have a job to get through the gap. Brian was nearly six feet tall and podgy too. But perhaps they could climb over.

Artie wasn't waiting to find out. He'd seen a place where he could hide, where they wouldn't find him, and he had just two minutes to reach it.

He pulled his zip up tighter, hardly leaving Bluey any breathing space but with no time now to bother about her comfort, and made a dash towards the tunnel which went underneath the big grey factory, taking part of the river with it. A narrow ledge ran along the tunnel wall, just wide enough for a person. Artie didn't know how far the tunnel went. He couldn't remember now where the river came out.

If he went in far enough his brothers wouldn't look for him but he'd have to go a good way, as far into the darkness as he dared.

It was all right at first because, although the day was gloomy and the rain still falling, enough light entered the tunnel to show him the way. The smell was horrible, rising up from the bubbles of frothy, factory waste on the water's surface. Soon the light became dimmer and dimmer and he couldn't see where he was putting his feet. He could hear his brother's voices. They were arguing, Brian convinced that he had seen him, Phil insisting it was only a dog.

Artie's pace became slower and slower. Darkness, complete and unbroken, lay ahead and his brothers' voices were muffled. Once he looked back at the dim grey light beyond the tunnel's mouth, and his heart leapt fearfully when he saw two figures standing there. Could they see him? Could they hear him?

'Art. Artie! We know you're there.' Silence. 'Come on out.' Silence. 'We're not going till you come out.' Again they waited for him to answer. 'Art!' This time it was Phil. 'You'll get drowned.' After a minute, 'There's rats in there, bigger than cats.'

But Artie wasn't being drawn. If they wanted him, they'd have to come and get him. Bluey's claws were digging through his T-shirt into his chest. She was terrified and he thought that any minute she'd let out a yowl. Luckily she wasn't given to making much noise and, while she clawed at him, remained silent.

He went forward a few more paces then halted, courage deserting him at last. He was now convinced that one more step would take him into the river itself, and imagined the black and grimy water closing over his head. There was the sound of drips and when he leaned against the wall for comfort in his shivery fear, it was clammy and slimy and stinking.

Artie thought he would die if his brothers didn't go away soon. He couldn't stand more of the darkness, the smell, and his growing fear of rats and drowning. He couldn't even feel Bluey's claws now because his body seemed turned to ice. He could still see Phil and Brian, distant, almost comforting figures, towards whom he was very much tempted to run, but abruptly they disappeared from sight and Artie almost gave a sob of relief.

He checked his desire to abandon the tunnel immediately. Perhaps they were waiting for him on the bank, expecting him to do just this. No. First he would count up to a thousand. That should be enough. Only when he'd counted a thousand would he make his way back to the open air.

One, two, three, four, five – he heard a scuffle and almost vomited with fright. Heart beating madly, nerves stretched to the limit, he listened. All he could hear was the blood thumping in his ears and he started counting again, his eyes shut.

13. Rain and weariness

As the hours went by and Artie didn't return home, Mrs Shaw grew crosser and crosser. Her anxiety of the previous night had been relieved when Phil and Brian told her of the chase Artie had led them until they lost him somewhere near the park. At least, in spite of his night out, he was all right and not far from home. But what was he doing? What was he thinking of?

When Jeff came back from the Play Centre in the afternoon she sent him to look for his brother. Reluctantly he returned to Abby's garden and, after knocking and calling in vain, found the key under the stone where Artie always hid it and opened the green gate. The shed door was open, the blue rug thrown in a pile just inside, and there was nothing to tell him whether or not Artie would be back. The rain had turned to a fine spray which soaked everything and the afternoon was so grey that it looked like night already. Jeff fingered a few things, looked at the pictures on the wall, sat in the cane chair for a minute or two then decided to go back home.

There was cottage pie for supper, as Mrs Shaw had stayed at home waiting for Artie and had done some cooking for a change, and nearly everyone was there to eat it because it was too miserable an evening for staying out. Sheila had gone to the pictures and Phil and Brian were supposed to be roaming the streets looking for Artie. Hardly anyone had anything to say, spirits damped by the tense atmosphere.

'What we going to do if 'e don't come 'ome tonight?' Mrs Shaw wanted to know.

'Oh don't worry. 'E'll be back. 'E won't stay out

another night in this weather,' her husband assured her between mouthfuls of potato and minced meat.

'We'll 'ave to tell the police if 'e don't come 'ome. I'm not taking any chances of 'aving 'im murdered or something. There's so many funny people about these days, you can never tell.'

'You just leave the police alone. The less we 'ave to do with them, the better. Just because the boy spends a couple of nights away from 'ome it don't mean you 'ave to call the police. 'E'll be back and when 'e gets through that door I'll give 'im a belting 'e won't forget in a 'urry.'

'But if he don't come back . . . ?'

Mrs Shaw's anger was changing to anxiety. Although she was careless of her children's welfare and rarely knew from one end of the day to the other where they could all be found, she had never had a child stay out all night and was imagining all sorts of terrible things happening to him.

''E's with that cat,' her husband assured her. 'No doubt looking for somewhere else to 'ide it. When 'e's found a new 'iding place, 'e'll be back. You'll see.'

But the night passed and Artie didn't return. The whole of the next day went by too, raining, windy, almost cold. This time Mrs Shaw accompanied Jeff to the garden but nothing was changed from the previous day. The shed door swung back and forth in the wind and a strange white cat watched them from the shelter of a gooseberry bush. All Artie's mother could say as she looked from the pictures to the suitcase with Bluey's bed, and saw the abandoned wheelchair with the wheels from Jason's fire-engine, was, 'Well I never. Well I never.'

She was beginning to realize just how much Artie felt for the cat he had found and to wonder at his determination.

That evening she had a row with her husband, who was

still against calling the police, and she marched out with her old green coat pulled up round her ears, wondering (as she hurried along to the station to report him missing) what Artie could be up to and how he was managing. Suppose he'd fallen in the river and drowned? Phil and Brian had seen him go in that direction. Suppose he'd got into some old house and fallen through a broken staircase and killed himself? Suppose someone who was odd in the head. . . .

She shook her head to drive away the horrible thoughts but she was almost in tears by the time the policeman at the duty desk had heard her tale. He had a cup of tea sent up from the canteen to console her and, while she was sipping it, set the wheels in motion for a general search.

*

It was just as wet down in Kent when Artie got off the train with Bluey well tucked inside his anorak, fast asleep. He had spent most of the journey trying to decide how to solve the problem of the train ticket. No one had asked for his ticket on the platform at Waterloo and there was no inspector on the train as Artie had expected. Therefore he supposed he would have to show his ticket at the final station.

The train wasn't very crowded. An elderly man sat in front of him reading a newspaper and didn't notice Bluey poking her head out from time to time to look out of the window. Artie had found a corner seat and spent most of the time watching the swiftly disappearing scenery, the London outskirts gradually giving way to more and more country. He expected to see lots of cows and pigs and chickens but, apart from the occasional grazing horse and a few huddles of sheep, the green, tree-lined fields were deserted.

He was feeling hungry and pulled out the milk chocolate he'd bought at Waterloo while waiting for the train. Bluey licked up a few crumbled bits from his fingers and the rest he kept for himself, sucking it slowly to make it last longer because it was all he was having for his dinner.

When he reached his destination, he was hoping to be able to outwit the ticket collector somehow or another but came face to face with this individual unexpectedly. He turned scarlet as he fumbled about in his pockets.

'I've lost it,' he said. 'Look. I got a 'ole in my pocket.'

The ticket collector just looked at him disbelievingly. 'Where did you get on, sonny?'

Artie thought quickly. 'Two stops back. But I did 'ave a ticket, honest I did.'

'What was the name of the station?' No rush, no anger in the round tones, just implacability.

He couldn't remember, of course, and after a few more inventions, which grew feebler each time, he handed over all that was left of the money in his pockets.

'I'll let you off this time, sonny,' said the ticket collector, giving him a receipt for his ten pence. 'It's an offence to travel on the railway without a ticket and you could be had up and taken to court. So don't do it again. I shall be watching out for you,' he warned.

'And with a cat too!' he added, as Bluey suddenly pushed her head out to see what was going on. 'I don't know. Go on with you, before I change my mind.'

Artie felt shaken after this encounter and walked about heedlessly for a while until his self-confidence returned.

'Trouble is, Bluey,' he said, in need of someone to talk to, 'we 'aven't got no money left for the bus. Still, I suppose we can walk, can't we?'

He fondled the cat's ears and Bluey rubbed her muzzle against him. She was looking a bit rough. The rain had dampened her hair considerably and so much travelling inside his anorak had rubbed her smooth coat in every direction.

'Never mind,' he went on, having pulled her out to inspect her and to let her stretch her front legs for a while. 'When we get to Abby's place we'll soon 'ave you cleaned up.'

By dint of asking, he found out which way the bus went and set off along the route which would take him to Abby. He had an awful lot of directions in his head, turn right at such and such a place, all the way up the hill, turn left somewhere else – or was it left the first time and right afterwards? Never mind, he'd ask again later on. Someone would be bound to know.

Artie soon left the main streets behind and then he was out in the country, with sloping fields on either side of him behind high, dripping hedges. It kept on raining, streaming into his face, creeping inside the neck of his anorak, soaking his tatty plimsolls and dirty socks.

'Poor old Bluey,' he said. 'But we'll soon be 'ome. Well,' he checked himself, 'it'll be 'ome for you, anyway.'

He fell silent, wishing he really was going home with Bluey and that he could keep her forever, but he pushed these thoughts away because they made him miserable.

Someone would be bound to know the way, but there was no one to ask. He kept on walking, following the lane along which hardly any traffic passed, tramping through mud and puddles. Bluey was getting tired of being squashed up inside his anorak for such a long time. She kept struggling to get out and began to mew impatiently, pulling herself up by her front legs, digging her claws into his chest and neck until at last he was forced to stop and give way to her.

He found a spot that was more or less protected by a lone

oak tree, growing among wild brambles. There was some flattened grass beneath the brambles where he put Bluey to keep her out of the rain and he sat down as near to her as he could, feeling for the first time the ache in his feet and legs and back. Bluey rubbed herself in the grass, purring with pleasure. She pulled at the brambles with her claws and chewed a few damp blades of grass with distasteful expression. Artie broke some up for her as she seemed to have difficulty in doing so herself and she ate them all, purring all the while.

'Course, it 'ad to rain,' sighed Artie with certain bitterness. 'It's been sunny all week but just 'cos we 'ave to make a journey it begins to rain.'

Bluey pulled at his hands with her soft paws, wanting to play, but Artie felt too miserable to respond and only half-heartedly noticed her.

'Come on,' he said at last. 'We'd better get a move on. It must be getting late and I got to get 'ome before it's dark. It's all right for you. You'll soon be warm and dry.'

He carried Bluey in his arms this time because she obviously didn't want to go back inside his anorak and, because she was getting wetter and wetter, he took off his jacket and put it round her. He was already soaked everywhere else so it wouldn't matter now if he got a bit wetter.

Bluey grew heavier and heavier. Artie followed the narrow, winding road, trying to ignore the pain that ran from his neck to his shoulders and down the middle of his back. Bluey kept climbing up towards his face, licking his wet cheeks in her caressing way and the scratches she unintentionally left began to sting in the rain, to add to the miserable itching of his sore legs.

When he climbed a hill he could see for a long way both ahead and behind him. There were a few houses beyond a small wood. Perhaps one of them was Abby's grandparents'. He pulled out the envelope to look at the address again.

A mist was creeping across the dark green fields, swallowing up hedges and furrows and making all landmarks indistinct. Perhaps it came from the sea, this chilling, threatening mist. He would hurry to those houses and ask the way. Someone would know. It couldn't be far now. He'd been walking for hours.

The houses he had seen were not near the roadside. A muddy lane, ridged with tractor tracks, led to them and

Artie took it, expecting to come upon the houses almost immediately. But they were almost half a mile away and when he had crossed the small wood, whose narrow paths were overgrown with ferns and bracken, he saw with sinking heart that the buildings were not houses at all, but stables or pig-sties. At least, this was all he could tell by the smell because the windows were all closed up and no animals were to be seen.

He saw a fellow trudging by with a bale of straw on his shoulder and ran to ask him if he were far from the place he sought, proffering the envelope, now damp and grubby, which the man screwed up his nose to read.

'You're a bit off the beaten track,' he said at last. 'If I'm not mistaken, this place is a good five miles from here. Yes. You've come the wrong way. The best thing you can do, if you don't want to be walking till nightfall, is cut across the fields. That'll take a good two miles off your journey, see.'

He paused to think then went on, 'Go back the way you've just come and a bit further up the main road, on the other side, you'll see a five-barred gate. Climb over that and then keep walking straight, straight as you can. You cross about three fields in a straight line and you'll come to another road. That's the one you want. Follow that and you'll come to where the buses run. And then it's only about a mile from there.'

Artie took all this in as best he could but his spirits drooped as he struggled with a feeling of defeat, utter weariness and an almost overwhelming sense of loneliness. Five miles! Or three across the fields! He bit his lip and twitched his nose. The man had already continued on his way, forgetting about him, so he turned back with a sigh, pulling Bluey up closer.

He hardly noticed where he was going, trudging on like

an automaton, aware only of the slicing rain and his growing weariness. In the middle of a field, with mist all round him and such a greyness everywhere that even the grass seemed to have lost its greenness, he stopped, momentarily unable to walk a step further with Bluey dragging him down. In that second he could have thrown her down, just to escape her heaviness and the responsibility that was turning sour, and then he felt sorely ashamed of the thought he had almost heeded and hugged her with a sob of despair.

Bluey made no response. She too was soaking wet and weary. Silent in her misery, unable to protest except with the occasional mew which Artie no longer even heard, she had resigned herself to her fate and was quite listless.

Artie started walking again, finding it difficult to cross the soggy fields, his feet sinking into the earth at every stride when they didn't slip and slide or trip over unseen stones. The road the man had talked about was no more than an illusion, an invisible hope which receded as his tiredness grew. He saw a tumbled-down cottage at the edge of a field and made his way over to it, hoping quite uselessly that someone might be there, expecting to find a bit of shelter at least.

There were only the outer walls, thick with nettles and high weeds, and an old-fashioned chimney-place whose iron ovens had grown rusty in the open air. There was also an old stone kennel with a length of rusty chain, half lost in the grass, but there was nowhere for Artie to shelter from the rain, which was driving still harder into his face.

Bluey stirred and mewed and it suddenly occurred to him that she at least could keep warm and dry for a while inside the old kennel. At least it would give him a rest from her and she would be comfortable.

He knelt down and felt inside the kennel. It was dry
and there was some old straw or grass in there which
would help to warm her. Carefully he placed her inside
the kennel, assuring her with words and caresses. She
didn't seem to mind. In fact she was relieved to be on
solid, dry ground again, sheltered from the wind and
incessant rain. She gave a short mew. It sounded like a
mew of thanks to Artie and at last a smile broke on his
lips.

'You'll be all right there, won't you?' he assured her.
'Wish I could get in there wiv you.'

While he wandered about the damp walls, seeking
shelter for himself and finding none, he began to wonder
if he could leave Bluey in the kennel while he found his
way alone to Abby's place. He could travel more swiftly
on his own and could no doubt be back within an hour
or so, with Abby for company, and even if he had to leave
her the whole night – because it was growing quite dark –
nothing could really happen to her.

She was warm and safe. No one could find her, nor
would anyone think of looking there. She might be a bit
hungry but she wouldn't die if she went without food
until tomorrow. Look how long she'd been in the tree, and
she hadn't died, had she?

The temptation to leave her, to find his way alone to
Abby's holiday address, became too great to ignore. He had
carried Bluey for hours. She was soaked through, just as
he was, and might catch a chill because the rain would
stay in her thick fur without drying. He would give her a
rub down with some of that dry grass inside the kennel
before he left her and then he would run all the way to the
road and to Abby's house.

No sooner was the decision made than Artie acted upon
it. He felt more cheerful now that he didn't need to worry

about Bluey, nor drag her weight with him any longer. He rubbed her all over with the brittle grass, which broke up and stuck to her fur, but got out the worst of the wet, and then he put his anorak on again and left her, promising to be back soon.

Before he went he took careful note of his surroundings so that he would remember where the house was. There was that big, dead tree over to the left, cleft down the middle by a stroke of lightning. As he looked about, he suddenly realized that he couldn't recall which way he had come towards the house. He had walked all round it before noticing the kennel but could no longer remember whether he had come from behind or in front. The fields all looked the same and didn't help at all.

He bit his lip, refusing to be overcome by this new misfortune then, deciding that if he had come from the direction of the dead tree he would have noticed it in passing, he must surely travel towards it now. The truth was that he couldn't recognize any of his surroundings and was completely lost.

But Artie wasn't one to give up in a crisis. He twitched his nose, shrugged his shoulders and went on walking. Sooner or later he'd come to a road and where there was a a road there were people or houses or something.

He trudged on and on and on, across fields, through hedges, over gates, and the mist closed in on him, making everything silent and invisible, even the gathering darkness. When he came to the road at last, he only recognized it by the feel of it under his feet. It was smooth after the uneven, soggy earth, and his heart leaped with joy. Soon now he'd get where he was going!

A car flashed by, almost blinding him with the glare of its headlights, and the darkness when it had passed was complete. But Artie went on walking, no longer caring

E

about the dark and the rain, no longer even feeling tired or lonely, nor even remembering the cat he had left at the abandoned cottage. His mind was a blank. His body was numb and when he dropped in exhaustion at the roadside, he didn't even know it.

14. Bluey alone

When Bluey realized that she was alone, when after listening carefully for some sound of Artie and hearing nothing but the wind blustering about the old building and the rain thudding on the slates above her head, she began to call. Her rare, occasional cry of want was lost on Artie, who was plodding across the soaked fields, and he mightn't have taken any notice even had he heard her.

She cried three or four times then waited, expecting him to return, and in the meantime watched the rain outside the kennel dancing on the beaten, grassy ground, her sharp ears pricked, her heart hopeful.

Tired of watching the rain, she looked up and about her, the fading light of day hardly entering sufficiently for her to see more than the darkness of the corners where spiders spun and beetles crept and other small creatures went about their business.

She began to feel warmer, drier, and licked her front paws industriously before starting on her shoulders and chest. She turned on one side and pummelled her under-parts, nibbling at the rough places with her tiny front teeth. Then she slept, worn out with the long, uncomfortable day.

Now and again her ears flicked as mysterious sounds registered in her subconscious; now and again her eyes opened momentarily. Once she woke with a start at the screech of an owl. All of her feeling body quivered with alertness but when the screech wasn't repeated and the only sound was the continued fall of rain, she went back to sleep, basking in the warmth of the sheltered place Artie had found for her.

The morning light was drear and feeble. The rain had

stopped but the wind blew showers of water from the nearby trees. Bluey peered from the interior of the kennel, instinctively cautious of her strange surroundings which she had forgotten overnight. She smelled strange scents. There was nothing she recognized, except the electric smell of the wet grass.

She dragged herself to the kennel doorway but the grass all about was heavy and tangled, in spite of the beating the rain had given it, and she was deterred from further effort. Hunger overwhelmed her. The day before she had eaten nothing but a few egg-soaked chips and some bits of chocolate. Where was Artie? Where was Abby? Where were all the things she knew that composed her day-to-day existence; the shed, the garden, the apple tree, the blackbird that tormented her with his song in the gooseberry bush? And once again she began to call, a soft, plaintive mew that grew into a positive howl of distress as the hours went by and no one heeded her.

A flock of gulls swooped across the sky, far above her, diving towards the fields and soaring upwards, and her green eyes gleamed and her claws dug into the earth as her hunter's instinct stirred.

Again she took refuge in sleep but this time her slumber was much disturbed because she was hungry and lonely and lost, and too soon she awoke to the sound of rain pattering down on the kennel roof, splashing onto her nose which was poking out from the doorway. She pulled herself in a bit and watched the rain. This time she did not cry out because she was well aware by now that the only beings were the distant birds or the crawling creatures in the darkness.

By the afternoon she had gathered sufficient self-confidence, induced mainly by hunger, to abandon her shelter. She didn't know where she was going. She just knew that she must seek some food and, in spite of the belligerent weather, she began to drag herself across the soggy ground with blind determination and hope.

Nose twitching, ears sharply questing, her direction was decided more by the lie of the ground than anything else. Where the grass was too high, where thistles or thick patches of wild flowers barred her way, she made patient detours. Not far beyond the ruins was a long line of hedge-row and she was intent on reaching it, instinctively aware that there must be shelter and some kind of prey among the roots and foliage.

It took her a long time to reach the hedge, but time meant nothing to Bluey. Now and then she stopped to rest, or her attention was caught by the gulls and other birds. From time to time the wind thrust so strongly against her that she was obliged to wait until it had passed. When at last she got there an early dusk was making long shadows across the field. A gleam of unexpected sunlight glowed on her mud-splashed coat, whose gloss had been Abby's pride.

With dusk, various small creatures began to venture from their hiding places and for a time Bluey just lay listening to their movements, lacking the experience to understand the meaning of the different sounds, though instinct raced to overtake the centuries of domesticity in her blood. An unwary field mouse stopped only a few paces away from her, little nose woffling in search of seeds or insects, and Bluey grew taught with anticipation. She had never been so close to any mouse before and, thanks to the down-wind, it would have been hers had she been able to make the one short, sharp leap required to fall upon it. Her helpless movement warned the mouse into instant escape and all Bluey could do was lick her anxious jaws and wait for another opportunity.

Throughout the night she hunted in the same frustrated fashion and it seemed that the little animals became aware of her helplessness for they ran about within inches of her nose and even stopped to take sharp glances at her. A cloudy moon gleamed feebly over the hills, faintly silhouetting the ruined house which was now too far away for Bluey to reach, not that she even remembered it because it held no associations for her.

Instinctively she drove herself northwards, following the hedge and its scuffling creatures until the rain began to pelt down again and she flattened herself against the earth, unprotected now, not even able to run for shelter. Her poor, weary body took all the fury of the sudden shower. She lay across a ridge, drenched and exhausted, unable even to drag herself from the puddle which formed about her hindquarters, not even aware of its coldness.

She flattened her ears against her narrow skull, she closed her eyes, and she let the elements do what they would with her body for she had neither will nor energy to care.

*

The road on which Artie had collapsed in exhaustion was little used, hardly more than a lane, and it wasn't until a cowman cycled up the hill on his way to work the next morning, at almost six o'clock, that he was discovered, soaked through and unconscious. The cowman was convinced that Artie had been the victim of a hit-and-run driver and called both police and ambulance from the farmhouse telephone, but when Artie was comfortably installed in the nearest hospital and the doctors had examined him from head to toe, it became apparent that there was nothing really wrong with him at all.

'I think he must have run away from home and tired himself out. He's got no money about him,' said the doctor to the policeman who was waiting to hear the results of the examination, 'so I expect he's had nothing to eat for a day or two. The only thing we found on him was this.'

He proffered the soggy, folded envelope, with Abby's handwriting hardly legible, so mixed was the ink with the rain that had seeped through his clothes.

'Hm,' deliberated the policeman. 'It could mean something I suppose. I'll get it looked into. We haven't had any notice of a missing boy lately but perhaps he hasn't been reported yet. Some of these parents. . . . ' He shook his head as if puzzled at the ways of parents. 'No signs of having been ill-treated, I suppose?'

The doctor shook his head. 'A few scratch marks, from a cat I should think. I think he just left home. An adventure, or a lark. You know what boys are.'

When Artie awoke it was with a tremendous hunger. He couldn't make out what he was doing in a hospital bed in a ward full of men, but vaguely the happenings of the previous day returned, as if he were remembering a dream. He remembered his tiredness and desperation, and he scratched his head and twitched his nose as he tried to make out how he happened to be in hospital.

A nurse filled in the missing details for him while she bustled about him, taking temperature and pulse and making him comfortable, and soon the doctor was examining him again, much to Artie's disgust because he didn't take kindly to being prodded about by strangers, and with the nurse watching too. But his mind was working quickly. They didn't seem to know where he'd come from or who he was. That meant they wouldn't know about Bluey either. Bluey! He started as he suddenly remembered how he had left her. Would she be all right? Would she still be there? And, more worrying still, would he be able to find her again, and would they let him?

'What's the matter?' asked the doctor, noticing his anxiety. 'Are you in some kind of trouble?' When Artie didn't answer he went on, 'At least you could tell me your name.'

'What for?'

'So I can write it on this chart. Then we'll know who it belongs to. We don't want to go mixing up your temperature with someone else's, do we?'

Artie just shrugged. He wasn't as dopey as all that! How old did the doctor think he was, anyway? Six?

'Can I 'ave somefink to eat,' he said. 'I'm 'ungry.'

The nurse smiled and promised to bring him some lunch very soon. Artie liked her better than the doctor. She didn't ask so many questions.

After lunch, which was a double helping of boiled bacon, mashed potatoes and greens, and a double helping of treacle tart, Artie felt a lot better. He also felt very sleepy. The crisp hospital sheets just invited his curling up in them, quite different to the ones at home which never smelled fresh and cool, and although he didn't mean to go to sleep he was soon soundly slumbering, dreaming of Bluey and the rain which was still sliding down the windows opposite his bed.

In the evening he had visitors, only one of whom he recognized.

'Abby!'

It was good to see her wide grin and hear her gay laughter. She introduced her grandparents, who were very curious to know him and didn't seem a bit grumpy, as were his own grandparents whom he only saw about twice a year, and who soon explained about the policeman who had called.

'We've been out all day and only found out about you an hour ago,' said Abby. 'I guessed it must be you. You're a scream. But what's happened? Tell me what's up.'

Artie soon explained the trouble he was in and how he had hoped her grandparents would look after Bluey. 'I don't suppose they'll really want to,' he ended, almost forlornly, 'but I didn't 'ave nowhere else to go, did I?'

'But where is Bluey? She wasn't with you when they found you. What have you done with her?'

'I've 'id her. She must be awful 'ungry. I'll 'ave to go and find her.'

'The first thing you'll have to do, young man, is let the police know where you live,' broke in Abby's grandfather. 'Have you thought how your parents must be worrying about you?'

Artie suddenly tightened his lips. 'I got to find Bluey first. I can't just leave 'er. If my Mum comes she'll take me back 'ome and that'll be that. When they going to let me out of 'ere, anyway?'

'I don't know. It depends on how you are, I suppose.'

'I'm all right. There's nuffink wrong wiv me.'

This was true. Artie hadn't even caught a cold in spite of his night in the rain and the utter weariness which had betrayed him at last. But the doctor insisted on his spending the night in hospital, just in case. He spent half an hour with Abby and her grandparents who at last persuaded him to give his address. Abby promised to look for Bluey and, best of all, her grandparents said that if his mother gave her consent he could spend a few days with them, at least until Bluey was found.

At last Artie began to feel cheerful, even though no one had promised to keep Bluey for him. Perhaps it was just the relief of no longer being entirely responsible for Bluey's fate and because his unquenchable faith told him that, once they had seen how beautiful she was, they couldn't possibly allow Mrs Bradley to kill her. At least he had

E*

some grown-ups on his side for a change, ready to listen to him, wanting to help him. This was something new. He described the ruined cottage as he remembered it and tried hard to remember exactly where it was, although this was much more difficult and they at last agreed that as soon as he was let out of hospital the best thing would be for him to show them the way he had come.

But early the next morning his mother arrived. All the trouble and anxiety Artie's escapade had caused had put her into a wicked temper, in spite of her relief at having found him safe and sound. She wouldn't hear of him troubling Abby's grandparents and when he was dressed almost dragged him out of the hospital, scolding him all the way to the station, all the way in the train, and not falling silent until they were back in London and on the Underground, going home.

Artie kept silent. He hardly listened to any of his mother's words, hardly even heard them, overcome with anxiety of his own. Abby didn't even know that he had been dragged away. Perhaps she'd think he didn't care. Would she keep her promise to look for Bluey? Suppose she couldn't find her on her own? Suppose she didn't even look?

Pale-faced, tight-lipped, he didn't even have anything to say to Jeff, who watched him awkwardly, not knowing how to talk to him, the gulf between them embarrassing them both.

Mrs Shaw's temper wasn't improved when Mrs Bradley turned up that afternoon, insisting that her cat should be immediately returned if she didn't want to have dealings with the police.

''Ere's the boy what took your cat,' she shouted, pushing Artie in front of her. 'If you want to know anything about that cat, ask 'im. I'm sick to death of the 'ole thing and don't want to 'ear no more about it. If that cat's so valuable, you ought to look after it better, that's what I say. Accusing my boy of stealing, when all 'e did was rescue it from a tree and try to look after it. Ask 'im where it is. I don't want to know. Ask 'im.'

She marched out of the room, shaking with rage, and Artie and Mrs Bradley could hear her slamming cups and plates about expressively. Mrs Bradley sat on the edge of a chair. There was a coat hanging from it but it was comparatively clear of objects. Artie stood there, sulkily hanging his head.

'Why don't you want me to have my cat back?' she said at last. 'There's so many cats you could have. Don't you realize how much my Sacha means to me?'

Artie didn't answer and so she went on, 'I suppose you think I'll have her put to sleep?'

He looked up belligerently. 'That's what you'd do, isn't it? It's what any grown-up would do, even Mr Fielding who's supposed to look after animals.'

'You could have given me a chance.' Instead of being angry, as Artie uncaringly expected, she seemed almost to be pleading. His look became one of suspicion.

'I might not have decided to destroy her. If you'd brought her back, there wouldn't have been so much trouble. All the expense I've been to! And I've been so unhappy, worrying about her. You've been a very unkind boy.'

Artie was stumped for a reply. He hadn't looked at himself in this light. Unkind? Something about Mrs Bradley's expression convinced him of her genuine unhappiness and he began to feel rather ashamed of himself, and rather foolish.

'Where is she now? Where have you hidden her? Let me have her back. Please.'

'I can't. I don't know where she is. That is, I know but my Mum won't let me go and find 'er,' and, with a burst of confidence, Artie poured out his adventures of the last couple of days and his fear that Abby alone would never be able to find the place where Bluey had been left.

'I think you'd better let me know where your little friend lives,' said Mrs Bradley when he'd finished. 'Perhaps she and I together can find Sacha, Bluey as you call her. Tell me again what the place was like. If your mother would only let you come!' She sighed. 'But I suppose she won't.'

Artie shook his head wryly.

'No. I thought not. Never mind. I'll find her. I shan't come back to London till I do.'

When she had gone, briskly determined now, Artie didn't know how to gauge his feelings. Did he want Mrs Bradley to find Bluey, or didn't he? And what was going to happen now?

15. Sacha again

Trudging about the muddy fields with rain-cap, overshoes and mac, all made of plastic, to protect her from the still occasional showers, Mrs Bradley wondered if she was being rather ridiculous, going to so much trouble for a cat. The search seemed so hopeless. Artie's directions were vague at the very best. The only true guide was the ruined cottage near the burnt-out tree, somewhere in the middle of a stretch of sloping, hedge-lined meadows, and so far neither she nor her willing companion, Abby, had found trace of either.

While she poked about among the bracken and brambles of the copses and ridges that crossed their path with a walking stick Abby's grandfather had lent her, her thoughts ran over the extravagance of this month-long search. The advertisements, the letters, and now the hotel bill for the days she stayed down here looking for a needle in a haystack. Was it worth it? Was there still any hope of finding her Russian Blue alive and, if so, in what condition would they find her?

The search for Sacha was in its third day and although the rain had dwindled to an occasional blustery shower and the sun forced its way through the clouds now and then, the air was damp and heavy and the ground did not dry out. If Sacha should still be in the old kennel, where Artie had left her, there might be hopes for her salvation. She would be ravenous but dry at least and reasonably warm. But supposing she had dragged herself away – this girl, Abby, had assured her of the cat's mobility – and was at the mercy of the weather or those gulls?

She looked up at the sky, where the grey and white

birds flocked and separated, swooping with frightening grace upon some unknown object in the distant furrows, cruel beaks open hungrily.

Their mews sounded like those of a cat in distress. At first they had misled her, causing her to rush from one place to another, certain that Sacha was calling her. And when she was puffed and red-faced and really feeling the years that had been insidiously overtaking her, she realized how the gulls had tricked her.

Abby was her tireless companion. If it hadn't been for that cheerful, hopeful, undaunted spirit, she would have given up at the end of the second day, too weary to feel any hope herself. But Abby ran ahead and ran back. She searched all the hedges of every field. She explored behind unexpected mounds, her long legs heedless of the rough, muddy ground which dragged at Mrs Bradley's tired limbs.

At last, when Mrs Bradley was thinking that she really must go back to the hotel for a hot bath, and perhaps get an evening train back to London, Abby gave a shout and began waving her arms excitedly. She was sitting astride the top bar of a five-barred gate and her whole expression was one of triumph.

'Mrs Bradley. Mrs Bradley. I've found it! I've found it. Quick. It's the ruined cottage.'

Mrs Bradley's heart gave a little leap of hope and she forgot about the hot bath and the twinges of rheumatism in her legs and shoulder as she caught something of Abby's excitement. The girl almost pulled her along to the old house but both their faces fell with disappointment when they found the kennel empty.

'It's no good, Abby,' sighed Mrs Bradley. 'I just can't go on. She could be anywhere. Anywhere'.

Defeatedly she stared beyond the trees whose leaves

shivered in the wind to the dead tree on the horizon, black and stark amid the deep summer colours. She had crossed so many fields, all deserted, and was beginning to think that if Artie hadn't dreamed this journey with the cat it might only be another tale of his to keep her from ever getting Sacha back.

'Oh, Mrs Bradley,' cried Abby, 'don't give up now. You rest here for a while if you like. I'll go on. I don't mind searching further.'

'But it's long past your tea-time. It must be nearly seven o'clock. Aren't you tired too, my dear?'

Abby shook her head fiercely. 'Not now we're so near to finding her. I'll just cross the field. She might be over in that hedge. There's a few trees beyond. Perhaps she's sheltering there.'

Mrs Bradley watched her rush off once more, envying her vitality, wishing she could share her hope. She sat down on a block of old bricks stuck together, with bits of grass growing out of the cracks, and wondered about the two children who had cared for Sacha so lovingly. She knew so little of children, having only vague memories of freckle-faced, fair-haired nieces of long ago. They were almost beings from another world, quite unconnected with her day-to-day life, and the few noisy, untidy examples of their species to be found any afternoon after school on the common had not encouraged her to think particularly well of any of them.

But first Artie, and now Abby, had set her wondering. They were human after all, with generous hearts and a sense of duty and sacrifice. Above all they had hope, bursting, bouncing, never-ending hope which could overcome every difficulty and make them blind to mountains crossing their path. Abby knew Sacha would be found, just as Artie knew that Sacha would want to live.

Really it was only because they wanted it to be so. It was only adults who accepted bitter facts and made the most of them. And Mrs Bradley sighed, wishing for just a moment that she might be a child again.

Abby had reached the hedge and was hurrying along it from edge to edge, expectant, eager, her very attitude holding back Mrs Bradley's creeping despair. But she found nothing. Sacha wasn't there. She watched her push through the hedge to the next field. There were a few trees not far off. Perhaps . . .

Ashamed of her own defeat, Mrs Bradley suddenly got up. She ought to be looking too, not leaving it all to Abby. She'd cross the field in the opposite direction. Perhaps . . .

It was a long, uphill trudge, through yielding, grass-covered earth that sucked at her overshoes, almost pulling them off. Halfway across she thought she saw . . . what was it? She didn't even know.

An old sack, a clump of wet newspaper, a dead gull?

She was tempted to ignore whatever it was for it was out of her way and hardly likely to be what she was looking for. But something prodded her into making the detour and as she got nearer both hope and fear began to pound in her tired body. It was! It couldn't be! It was only an old rag from a scarecrow. It couldn't be Sacha! But suppose . . .

And when she was there, standing over it, hardly daring to look down, too afraid to accept the awful truth that this was the end of her beautiful cat, her affectionate, good-natured Sacha, her greatest longing was to have Abby beside her, to have someone to hold on to, who cared as much as she did. But Abby was almost out of sight, far beyond the distant hedge, and didn't even know that Sacha was here, at her feet, crushed by the rain, the mud, neglect and helplessness.

After the first shock, the first curl of pity and misery inside her, she noticed that Sacha's eyes were shut. In spite of the battered aspect of the once sleek, blue-shining body, there was not altogether the look of death about her. Mrs Bradley had seen dead cats in the road, frigid, taut, eyes glassy, staring. There was a limpness about this abandoned thing at her feet which suggested a tremble of life, a hope not entirely stamped out.

Not daring to believe, almost afraid to, she leaned over the inert body and gathered it into her arms. 'Oh, you poor, poor thing,' she exclaimed softly. 'Who would ever have believed. . . . ' and again, 'You poor, poor thing.'

She went back to the ruined house and sat on the broken masonry as before, nursing the nearly lifeless cat in her arms and waiting for Abby to return. She massaged the poor body with urgent fingers, trying to encourage the flickering, fading warmth and while she worked and waited she told herself, 'She's got to live. I won't let her die. I won't. I won't.'

*

A whole week went by during which Mrs Shaw hardly let Artie out of her sight, a most unusual event which upset all the family routine. He went with Jeff and the other children down to the Play Centre every day, where he was dished up a school dinner and left to wander in solitary fashion about the half-deserted playground for the rest of the time. Jeff tentatively accompanied him but Artie was still sore. Jeff's treachery was hard to get over. As far as he knew Bluey was lost, as good as dead, and he still felt that it was his brother's fault.

When Jeff asked him about his adventures his sharp reply was, 'What you want to know for?' and after a few more similarly brusque answers, Jeff went back to the school library to lose himself in a new adventure story.

Artie didn't know what to do with himself. Bluey had been his whole existence for more than a month. He had woken up thinking of her and gone to sleep to dream of her and all his waking hours had been devoted entirely to her care. Any way of life he had known before Bluey came to share his days was completely forgotten, the park, the common, the swimming pool, even Freddie, the dog he had always wanted and could never have.

He felt as though a bit of himself had been cut right out, sharply, cruelly, leaving him still inwardly bleeding.

Once he went back to Abby's garden. The back gate was unlocked and when he pushed it open and stood on the first bit of unkempt lawn, surveying the shed, the apple tree and the back of the house with its many drainpipes, he was swamped by a strange sensation. As if nothing were real, as if everything had been only a dream.

He went to the shed and looked at the cat pictures on the wall. There was Bluey's bed in the old suitcase; there was the blue rug, just as he'd left it, tumbled on the floor, and the basket chair where Abby would sit and nurse Bluey on her knees. Wildly he dragged all the pictures off the wall, screwed them up and threw them on the floor, then he slammed out of the shed, out of the garden, and went running, running home.

At the end of the week the postman brought a letter, a surprising event because the only things that were ever dropped through their letter box were the weekly football pools and the occasional advertisement. No one ever wrote any letters. But there it was, addressed in clear round letters to 'Master Arthur Shaw'.

'Cor blimey!' exclaimed his mother. 'We are going up in the world, aren't we! Master Shaw you are now. Soon we'll 'ave to pay a tanner to talk to you.'

But she was as curious as everyone else to know who it

was from and amid a huddled circle of onlookers, Artie opened his very first letter.

It was from Abby. She told him all about the search for Bluey and how Mrs Bradley had eventually found her and taken her back to London. 'She said she would get in touch with you so perhaps you already know all this,' she finished.

'That blessed cat!' exclaimed his mother. 'Seems like you're never to 'ear the end of that story. When I think of all the trouble you've caused, just for a blooming cat!'

But Artie wasn't even listening to her. His heart had opened once again with hope and gladness at Abby's news and the misery knotted inside him all week had disappeared. He almost jumped in the air with joy and didn't care when someone snatched the letter from his hand. He swung round, his pinched face suddenly alight again, looking for Jeff.

'Did you 'ear what it said?' he cried, giving him a friendly punch on the arm. 'Bluey's alive and that Mrs Bradley's looking after 'er.'

'I knew 'e'd be all right,' grinned Jeff, who still hadn't got into the habit of calling her 'she'. 'Cats are supposed to 'ave nine lives, anyway.'

With this they started a discussion as to how many lives Bluey must have spent already and, by the time they had come to an agreement, Artie had forgotten his bitterness towards his brother and Jeff was no longer feeling that he had been too harshly judged.

They went to the park because they had nothing else to do and talked about Bluey most of the time, how Artie had found her, how she'd pulled the curtain down in their room and made such a mess of their mother's geranium, and whenever they saw a cat they exclaimed, 'Cor! That one's not a patch on Bluey.' What cat ever could be?

The fat beagle was in the park and obligingly ran after a few sticks thrown for him by Artie. Then a hairy, long-tailed mongrel came gambolling to join the game, throwing himself on Artie with boisterous delight, almost knocking him over. Artie's grin nearly stretched from ear to ear as the mongrel slobbered his pink tongue all over his face and round his neck.

'Dogs are best,' stated Jeff, watching his brother dancing around with both of them. 'You can't play like that wiv a cat.'

'Who says?' began Artie belligerently, but the mongrel threw itself on him again, this time getting him on the ground and awkwardly straddling him to lick his ears and pull at his patchy clothes, while Artie shouted delightedly and hardly tried to keep the dog at bay.

The mongrel dashed away as unexpectedly as he had come and Artie watched after him regretfully.

'I wouldn't 'alf like to 'ave a dog like that,' he sighed. 'If I win the football pools one day when I grow up, that's just the sort of dog I'm going to 'ave.'

*

Meanwhile, Bluey – or Sacha as she was properly named – was fighting for her life. Mrs Bradley had called the vet, a middle-aged man who had looked after her animals for years, vaccinating her dogs, treating them for minor ailments, and once performing a major operation on a Jack Russell terrier that had swallowed a needle. When he saw the Russian Blue, which he remembered as a slender, playful kitten not so very long ago, sinking slowly but irremediably from life, his dismay was genuine.

He already knew that she had been lost and Mrs Bradley quickly filled in what she knew of her adventures, especially those of the last few days. When she told him that he must do absolutely everything in his power to save her, he was not only doubtful but surprised. Mrs Bradley had never held on to a suffering animal for which hope had been quite surrendered and had more than once said that animals were luckier than humans in that they could be painlessly destroyed when life became a burden to them.

Yet now she was asking him to save this miserable, crippled, hopeless animal, already far nearer to death than life, and begging him, with almost childish hope, to assure her that it could be done.

With pursed lips, stethoscope and skilful hands, he felt his way about the yielding frame, doubtfully registering the quivering heartbeats, frowning at the temperature of the fevered body. At last he said, 'I can give her some medicine which might or might not help but what she needs most of all is careful, devoted nursing – night and day – if you're to bring her through. It's not so much what I can do, but what you must do if you want to save her.'

With this, Mrs Bradley was satisfied. She had the example of the two children's devotion and since knowing them had contracted their belief and hope. When she was tired, she brushed the feeling away. For hours and hours she watched the Russian Blue's slightest movements, kept her warm with constantly renewed hot water bottles under a soft blanket, kept her clean with cotton wool and gentle brushing, kept her fed with drips of sweetened milk or warm Bovril.

She had promised Abby she would write to Artie but the days went by, and most of the nights as well, when she had no time to think of anything but the hardly moving Sacha. Once she began a letter to Artie, sitting in an armchair with the cat at her feet in a basket beside the gas fire, but she found she didn't know what to say and left it.

Then one day, she didn't know how many days after she had brought her home – only that the vet had called four times and marvelled at the fact that she was still clinging so precariously to her crippled life – Sacha's green eyes stared fully at her with a look of recognition in them that was beyond questioning. The long ears suddenly pricked, the whiskers quivered, a short rasping sound came from the throat that had been still and quiet for so long.

Mrs Bradley fell to her knees beside the basket, caressing the brittle-haired skull, rubbing her fingers softly up and down Sacha's chin and throat, gently murmuring grateful words.

After that, Sacha's progress became more obvious. Soon she was tired of milk and Bovril and progressed to solid food, and then she was struggling to get out of the basket, scornful now of the hot water bottles that had kept the faint heart beating, determined to live her own life again, quite unaware that she was supposed to be still convalescent.

She remembered her old home and was obviously pleased to recognize the different corners and bits of furniture. Once she dragged herself all along the passage towards the kitchen and back garden and, as it was a warm day, Mrs Bradley took her outside and put her down on the grass.

Sacha began to play. She couldn't play as Mrs Bradley remembered, whole body writhing with energy and joy, the long tail whipping or quivering expressively. Those long back legs were two bits of limp immobility, reminding her of the still warm corpse of a rabbit which a dog of hers had dragged home from the hills of a country home, its legs dangling from either side of its mouth. But she half-rolled on her back and clawed at the daisies near her head and all the live half of her was intensely alert when the blackbird who lived near the chimney pot suddenly burst into song.

Watching her like this, it came to her that Artie had been quite right to keep the cat away from her. Had he brought her back that first day, still dazed from the accident, so newly crushed and helpless, her first reaction would have been to have her immediately destroyed. She knew this without the slightest doubt.

People, herself included, had the habit of endowing their animals with their own thoughts and feelings and it had taken a child to show her that this was wrong. Sacha didn't mind about her crippled body. She lived within its

bounds quite happily, much more happily than any sensitive human would have supposed. The main thing was to be alive, to be able to hear the blackbird sing and still expect to hunt it one day; to pretend the grass was a fearsome enemy; to listen to the wind rush through the trees or bask in front of the gas fire on a chilly evening, eyes half closed, with the comfort of a full stomach and a friendly voice or hand not far away.

She had no memory of yesterdays, no expectation of tomorrows, so what human being had the right to take away her todays of every day?

At last she wrote to Artie and asked him to come and see her. On the day she expected him, she brought him a present because she knew she owed him so much and that she had taken away what was probably the very best thing he'd ever had. She brought him one of the puppies from the grocer's shop, a little black and white mongrel with pricked ears and a long curly tail which seemed quite ridiculous to Mrs Bradley.

'It's Freddie!' cried Artie when he saw him. 'Look, Jeff, it's just like my Freddie,' because when Artie took the puppy in his arms and let it lick and wriggle all over him, it was for him the invisible Freddie who had accompanied him on so many occasions in the park and on the common.

'But you can't take 'im 'ome,' warned the ever-practical Jeff who knew nothing about Freddie and didn't know what Artie was talking about.

'I will,' cried Artie. 'I don't care what Mum says. Mrs Bradley's given 'im to me. 'Aven't you?' he appealed to her.

'Well, yes, but if you can't keep animals. . . . ' She paused. 'It's rather awkward. I can't very well take him back to the shop.'

'I'll 'ave 'im. I'll 'ave 'im.'

Artie's face was scarlet with emotion. He couldn't bear to be parted from this sharp-toothed, bright-eyed, bouncing puppy, although it had only been his for the last ten minutes. He had almost forgotten about Bluey, who was watching the proceedings somewhat disdainfully, although she couldn't quite resist her curiosity for the new little animal. He knew she was well, he knew Mrs Bradley meant to keep her, and all that mattered now was that he should be allowed to keep his Freddie.

At last Mrs Bradley smiled and said, 'I have an idea. If you can't keep Freddie at home, why don't you keep him here?'

Artie looked glum. Somewhat awkwardly, not wanting to appear ungrateful, he said, 'But like that 'e wouldn't be my dog, would 'e? I mean, 'e wouldn't love me best, would 'e?'

'Oh yes he would because you would have to look after him and take him for walks and everything. I'm too old now to look after puppies. You can even buy his food, so that you can really be responsible for him, and give it to him yourself. Like that he'll know you're his master.'

Artie twitched his nose thoughtfully. 'If you think it'll be all right,' he accepted.

She smiled.

'And can I come for 'im whenever I like? And can Jeff come wiv me? And can I play wiv Bluey sometimes? I mean, if I'm 'ere I got to see 'er, 'aven't I? I can't 'elp seeing 'er, can I?'

'You can come whenever you want to and bring your brother, and Abby too. It's good to have young people about. I didn't realize it before. That's why I'm getting so old, because I've no one young to talk to.'

'Oh no, you're not old,' argued Artie gallantly. 'Not really. Not like some people I know, anyway.'

Mrs Bradley had prepared the kind of tea she thought Artie and Jeff would like, with lots of chocolate and creamy cakes, and a trifle and strawberry jelly. Freddie sampled bits of everything and left quite a few smudges and wet bits over the carpet but Mrs Bradley said it didn't matter. Then she told them to take him for a walk on the common and watched them from her front window, with Bluey in her arms, as they hurried over to the green, Artie's face alight with happiness, Jeff grinning, and the puppy barking sharply at them both in turn.

Mr Hinton
17 Seafield Close
East Battering
Sussex